"I AM NOT JUST AN EMPTY-HEADED FEMALE READY TO SUCCUMB TO THE TYRANNY OF MARRIAGE. I WANT RESPECT FOR MY MIND."

This was the explosive beginning of Merry's rebellion against marriage. It led her to consider a most disturbing and titillating proposition—involving a man she had never met....

Fawcett Crest Books
by Audrey Blanshard:

THE FRENSHAM INHERITANCE

GRANBOROUGH'S FILLY

THE SHY YOUNG DENBURY

A VIRGINIAN AT VENNCOMBE

THE SHY YOUNG DENBURY

Audrey Blanshard

A FAWCETT CREST BOOK • NEW YORK

THE SHY YOUNG DENBURY

Published by Fawcett Crest Books, a unit of CBS Publications, the Consumer Publishing Division of CBS Inc., by arrangement with Robert Hale Limited

ISBN: 0-449-23666-8

A selection of the Doubleday Romance Library

Printed in the United States of America

10 9 8 7 6 5 4 3 2 1

Before Almeria Denbury (known to her intimates as Merry) opened the large gilded mahogany door to the drawing-room, she took a deep breath, but first burying her face in a lawn handkerchief generously imbued with her sister's latest toilet water, 'Sans Pareille'. Not that the Denbury mansion in Bedford Square was in any way more noisome than its neighbours; the fact was that in the oppressive heat of an August afternoon the multifarious odours of London seemed to penetrate every corner of even such an outlying dwelling as theirs.

But, in any event, a deep steadying breath was

always a wise prelude to an interview with her mother. Not giving herself time to speculate on the reason for the summons she pressed the handle; a welcome draught, created by the door's opening, felt almost cool through Almeria's flimsy India muslin gown.

"Ah, better late than never!" Mrs Denbury's voice cut across the heavy atmosphere with an amazing briskness. "There's no call to slam the door, Almeria. Come and sit down." She raised her capped auburn head and looked closely at the girl. "Your hair cannot have been dressed since you rose this morning." Then she sniffed ostentatiously. "What trashy scent is that?"

Jane Denbury had the sort of strong handsome features which shed none of their attraction with maturity: she was charming and amusing to her contemporaries but could be formidable to the young—and particularly to Almeria. Her criticism of her youngest daughter had become so habitual over the years she scarcely noticed it; the same could not be said of Almeria, although on this occasion she was relieved there were no witnesses for the reproofs.

Merry knew, of course, that the last peevish question was automatic and rhetorical. If her mama had been aware that it was Theodosia's scent it would have been everything that was delightful. So, she sat facing her parent in silence in the spacious apartment furnished in the fashionable Egyptian style.

The Denburys had spent much of their early married years in India, and this had given Mrs Denbury a lingering taste for the exotic. It had also, apparently, rendered her impervious to heat, reflected her daughter with a touch of envy: her mama looked wonderfully cool sitting bolt upright on the scroll-ended modern sofa, made more for elegance than comfort. The gold light filtered through the curtains drawn against the sun and for a brief fanciful moment Almeria, much influenced in her formative years by a succession of governesses who had followed the vogue for instilling the history of ancient civilizations into their charges, fancied herself in some Egyptian temple, before the throne of Isis herself perhaps . . . Absently she clasped the gilt sphinxes on the arms of her chair. But no, she thought, her plain common-sense quickly asserting itself, her mama could scarcely be regarded as a goddess of fecundity having only three daughters to her credit. Indeed, poor Queen Charlotte with her fifteen offspring might—

"Almeria! I did not ask you up so that you may sink into one of your trances like a drugged dormouse."

"No, mama." She withdrew her hands from the cool brass and folded them meekly in her lap; she tried to look alert.

"The fact is I am giving a dinner-party on Friday for just a few special friends."

Merry knew this already so why the hint of hesitation in her mama's usual assured manner, she wondered.

Mrs Denbury appeared engrossed in smoothing the quilling at her wrist. "Mr Jonathan Tiffen will be of the party."

Almeria gave an unladylike gurgle of laughter. "Oh no, mama!" Small wonder she hesitated to divulge that, she thought. "Not one of **the** bug-destroyer Tiffens! How famous!"

Mrs Denbury drew in her breath sharply. "If that is an example of the general tone of your conversation one should be grateful that in company you are unfailingly as dumb as a dancing-bear," she concluded, with one of her more colourful images.

Almeria had a passion for reading and for the assimilation of useless titbits of information: the revelation of a hitherto unknown fact such as this was the only thing which could have made her heedless of drawing more criticism upon her head. "Are they really, mama? Dumb, I mean. I should have thought—"

"You should have thought a great many things," retorted Mrs Denbury tartly, and in some danger now of becoming as heated as everyone else in the oppressively hot weather. "Mr Jonathan Tiffen," she went on, shifting a little on the hard golden cushion, "has no connexion whatsoever with Tiffen, the—the bug-catcher—and I cannot call to mind anyone but you who would have the indelicacy to think so—let alone give expression to the thought. However, it is no great wonder to me that you should greet my attempts to introduce the subject of your marriage with little short of ridicule." She had not intended this to be such a bald announcement; the truth was she found her youngest daughter wholly exasperating, had little patience with her quiet studious ways, and was constantly goaded into ill-considered remarks. Added to which, she had been rehearsing this particular interview all morning. She attempted to ameliorate her unfortunate mistake.

She did so in typical fashion, whilst Almeria steeled herself for one of her mama's periodic lectures on the desirability of an early marriage, and her complete failure to achieve that aim during her first London season; which, to Merry's enormous relief, was now over for another year.

"There now, it is quite impossible to converse with you when you respond in such an unseemly manner," her mama was saying. "It was my wish merely to acquaint you with your papa's decision to accept Mr Tiffen's offer for your hand and to encourage him in his suit."

"Offer?" cried Merry, alarm lending strength to her normally soft voice, "but I've never heard of him!"

"Well, he has heard of you, and seen you under this very roof, I may say. Although it is no surprise that you are in ignorance of his existence, as you choose to cultivate that arrogant shyness of yours."

"Oh, I don't, mama! I cannot help myself. When

I see strange faces at any gathering my mind goes quite blank."

"I am well aware of that," Mrs Denbury acknowledged scathingly, "and if you will succumb to the headache when there is an important entertainment, it is not to be supposed that the strange faces will ever be any other than strange to you." She reached for a round, gaudily-painted fan at her side and, whilst plying it in a measured fashion, said: "You will *not* take refuge in the headache on Friday, or in any other frippery excuse. Mr Tiffen naturally wishes to further his acquaintance with you at the earliest opportunity, and I thought it better you should meet in company for a while before he pays his address to you alone."

Almeria was frantically searching her memory for any feature or mannerism connected with the name Tiffen: but she was sure it was a name she had not heard before for, if she had, she would quite likely have disgraced herself by blurting out something about the bug-catcher. That was the difficulty in meeting new people, one could not say the first thing that came into one's head, so it was easier to stay silent, she found. Not surprisingly, she brushed aside her parent's calm plans for furthering their non-existent relationship.

"Mama, who is he?" she enquired in anguished tones. "How old is he? What does he look like? If you describe him I may be able to recognise him." She would not marry him, of course, whoever he was. She was only eighteen but would rather run away—anything. . . .

"Well, at least I hope it may teach you to take more heed of your fellows." Mrs Denbury did not appear in any way moved by her daughter's agitation, and went on reflectively, "Let me see, he is about two-and-twenty, I fancy; destined for the church—an excellent living has been found for him in Hampshire. But he is in possession of a comfortable income, and has expectations of an uncle, I believe, so you need entertain no fears on that score."

"The church? Hampshire?" reiterated Almeria blankly, the gentleman's financial standing at this stage being the last thing to worry her.

Mrs Denbury shook her head. "I fear I can have very little sympathy with you, you know," she observed somewhat unnecessarily. "Had you shown the least interest during these past months in fixing upon a husband of your own choosing, I should not have been driven to these lengths."

"But I have not *driven* anyone! How should I when I have no wish to marry?" Almeria felt on the verge of tears with the injustice of it all, and did not trust her voice further.

"There is no reason whatever why you should not marry. Indeed, it is plain as a pikestaff to me that it is the only thing which will compel you to lift your head from your interminable books. It is a most unhealthy preoccupation, and would give a more robust girl than you the headache, I vow."

Almeria abandoned her quest for the identification of her future husband: she must at once seek out her cousin, Frances, her only ally in an alien household—except perhaps for her father, although he did not appear as an ally on this occasion.

She had just risen rather precipitately prior to making her escape when her father entered.

Robert Denbury had not severed his early close links with the East India Company entirely, and if he was from home, as he frequently was, East India House in Leadenhall Street was the most likely place to discover him. He had been there that afternoon.

"Ah, by George, it's devilish warm today, couldn't abide the bustle and stink of the city," he exclaimed in his blunt way. "For once I'm glad to live out of the world here, hard by open fields." He walked over to the tall sash windows and jerked back the curtains letting in a flood of sunlight. "A cry of mad dog went up in Cheapside as I drove home—only to be expected in this weather, I suppose."

Even this alarming intelligence did not divert his wife from the matter in hand. "I have this minute been telling Almeria of her good fortune," she announced without preamble.

Mr Denbury, who had been mopping his brow, turned about at hearing this. "Bless my soul, didn't see you standing there, Merry!" he exclaimed, one eye temporarily obliterated under the large handkerchief. "And what have you to say to Jonathan Tiffen, then?"

"What can I say since I do not know the gentleman?" The indignation had died away now and, in any event, she felt sure her father had played a lesser part in arranging the match than her mother.

"How's this? Don't know him? To be sure you must do, child. Stocky dark fellow, eyes a bit too close together for my taste—but there it is, we don't choose our faces, do we? Has a stammer like a Brunswick—seems to be always under my roof sharing my dinner. You must know him."

As a description of a prospective husband it was not without its infelicities, but it served its purpose nonetheless—as her mother's efforts had not. Merry recognised Jonathan Tiffen at once, and her spirits reached their lowest ebb. She had never had the least desire to affix a name to the solemn young man with the slight stammer, and with whom she had not conversed at all. "Oh," she said faintly, "yes."

"Of course you do," rejoined her father, undaunted by the appalled tone of the response—if he noticed it at all. "You'll make a splendid pair," he commented, as if they were carriage horses. "Both bookish, quiet—admirably suited to a peaceful parsonage life deep in the country, a hundred miles away."

His wife echoed these sentiments warmly, as well

she might as she had implanted them in the first place. However, she tried hastily to modify the picture of far-flung isolation suggested by her over-enthusiastic spouse. "You have always had a fancy for country life, Almeria, and on many occasions have expressed your distaste for the hubbub of London."

This was true, but it was the particular hubbub of the husband-seeking parties and balls she really meant, and the alternative Almeria had envisaged somewhat wistfully, from time to time, had not included a bleak parsonage to be shared for life with one of the dullest young men she had ever seen: rather, she had pictured herself in a dear little thatched cottage, not too far away, Wimbledon perhaps, or even in a spick-and-span little villa at Muswell Hill—and then only for a few months in the year. As to taking charge of the smooth running of a country establishment and assuming the role of a vicar's wife (of whose duties she had only the haziest notion, although she suspected being bookish would not be of paramount importance to them) her mind boggled at the prospect.

All this and more passed through her head in a confused manner until suddenly one puzzling fact occurred to her. So, of course, she found herself blurting it out. "How can Mr Tiffen possibly preach sermons if he stammers?"

Her mother, who had been anticipating at the very least agreement that a rural life would be most welcome to her daughter, looked surprised and then disgusted. She resorted to her fan once more, but Mr Denbury gave an appreciative snort.

"Ha! Prove a great asset, I shouldn't wonder. Keep the congregation on the edge of their pews with excitement wondering what the next word is going to be!"

Mrs Denbury, now thoroughly exacerbated, astonished her husband by including him in her criticism. "Please, I beg you, don't encourage the child in her regrettable habits." She turned to Almeria, grim-faced. "You had best go and reflect quietly on this news. I can see it has quite overset you, which was only to be expected, I suppose—"

This sounded as if it might herald a sympathetic end to the interview but Almeria knew better than to expect such a reaction from her mother.

"—you have always been a high-strung, stubborn and ungrateful girl."

With these words ringing in her ears she finally escaped leaving her father mildly remonstrating with his wife.

Almeria made her way down the broad curving marble stairway, intent upon finding her cousin, Frances, who must have returned from her shopping expedition by this time, she thought: she would try the morning-room first.

As she turned the corner and set her foot on the last flight down to the hallway, Frances, who had obviously just come home, was handing some packages to the footman.

"See that cook has these at once—oh, no, not that one—I'll keep that." She glanced up briefly at the girl coming down the stairs. "Hallo, Merry. Mustn't send the *Lady's Magazine* to the kitchen, must I? You'd never forgive me. You'll be wanting to read the latest instalment of the serial, I daresay." She was clad in a lilac sarcenet gown of no great substance and a diaphanous silk shawl, but even so she quickly put off the shawl. "Be a dear and carry these for me, would you, Merry?" Almeria took the magazine and the shawl absentmindedly as her cousin went on: "I would not have believed it possible that silk should feel so stifling."

They were at the door of the morning-room now and Frances paused and looked enquiringly at her cousin. "You've not said a word. Anything wrong?"

Merry opened the door for her. "Please, not a lecture from you, too, on my shy and retiring ways!"

"As if I could!" laughed Frances. "You are not so with me. So," she said as she stripped off her kid gloves, "you'd better tell me all about it, but first ring for some lemonade, I'm quite parched."

Mrs Frances Wren had come to live with the Denbury family three years before, shortly after her husband, Captain Wren, had been killed in Spain at the battle of Cuidad Rodrigo. She was only five-and-twenty now, and in spite of Merry being the youngest Denbury sister she quickly attached herself to her cousin: they were now bosom-friends.

Indeed, to the stranger they had the strong appearance of sisters: both had fair complexions and hair, Merry's being a shade richer honey-gold than that of her widowed cousin; and now that Merry had been able to let her slightly-waved hair grow long from the school-room crop of earlier days, they both affected a smooth chignon style—embellished with a fashionable *frisette* of curls at the forehead for formal occasions. The young girl's golden looks were enhanced by beautiful amber-coloured eyes and well-defined brows: the modelling of her features, unremarkable in itself, was thus saved from the commonplace by the striking coloration.

Merry's real sisters, Theodosia and Cordelia, on the other hand, each had dark curly hair, vivid complexions and treacle-brown eyes, and with dispositions as buoyant and effusive as Merry's was quiet and retiring. The difference between the girls was marked enough to have set tattlemongers' tongues a-wagging on occasion, and even Merry herself, as soon as she knew Frances well enough, had raised the matter with her, albeit somewhat tentatively.

"Fanny," she had said one day, whilst her cousin was bent over her needlework and she looked out of the window, "it is odd, is it not, that my sisters and I should be so wholly dissimilar?"

"Oh, I don't think so. It happens like that sometimes."

"Mm, I suppose it does," she acknowledged dissatisfied, "but sometimes I don't *feel* I'm their sister at all."

"Well, you are, and there's an end to it," Frances said prosaically.

There was a pause. "You don't think I could be a . . . *half*-sister?"

"Really, Merry, I believe you do read too many novels, as your mama says! How could you blacken her name in that fashion?"

"Cordelia and Theo were both born in India, you know," Almeria persisted. "And I didn't arrive until the family were fixed in London, so it could be that—"

"Nonsense! If you cherish some fanciful notion of being a nobleman's illicit daughter you are sadly out, I am sure! A more devoted couple than your parents I have never seen. No! I think you could as likely attribute your sisters' darker colouring to their being born in a hot climate! Besides," Frances concluded, "you have a quite distinct look of your father *and* more than your fair share of his York-shire forthrightness—when you can overcome your reticence—as I know!"

Almeria had been finally satisfied and forgot her suspicions, but their dissimilar appearances and characteristics remained and she still felt overshad-owed and a little in awe of her sisters. In her present situation she certainly envied them, as she confided to Fanny over the lemonade.

"If only, when I came out this spring, I could have turned overnight into an accomplished flirt like Theo, I should not be faced with this dreadful *fait accompli* of mama's."

Frances permitted her youngish features a matronly frown of disapproval. "I don't believe a young lady should become a flirt overnight just because she is out, but certainly she is expected to turn from a demure, unassuming creature into an assured young woman, able to conduct herself with all the polish of one twice her years. It *is* difficult," she conceded.

"No, it is not, it's impossible—for me, in any event," Almeria said in a morose voice. "I have no wish to talk a great deal of silly nonsense to a host of unfamiliar young men whom I have never seen before and will most likely never see again."

"You have to see Mr Tiffen again, though, there is no avoiding *that*," Frances reminded her.

"Is there no way I can contrive to miss this beastly dinner on Friday?" she asked in a beseeching voice.

"None, Merry," Frances said with uncharacteristic sharpness. "Consider poor Mr Tiffen's feelings."

"I am doing so," objected Merry. "He will suffer the less if he is repulsed now rather than later."

"But you may not wish to repulse him. You confess you scarcely know him, although how that comes to be when you must have been in the same room with him several times, I do not know! But there, I know how timid you can be in company. You should strive to overcome this tendency," Frances urged kindly, rising to replace her empty glass on the tray. "An excess of modesty can bespeak a degree of pride and arrogance."

Merry looked disconsolate. "Mama said almost the same thing. It's not true, I'm not arrogant."

"*I* know you're not, but others don't. Still," she said bracingly, as she resumed her seat, "Mr Tiffen can't think you so if he wishes to marry you. I'm sure you will like him, he is a pleasant, gentleman-like man. I spoke with him for some time one evening when most of the company were at the tables. I own I found him to have a most open-temper—and such kind eyes," she added inconsequentially.

Almeria ignored these recommendations. "Theo says no man under five feet nine is gentleman-like."

Frances smiled. "Well, I must own, I did not have my measuring-tape at hand, but he stands several inches taller than I—and you—which is the chief concern, surely."

"But his stammer, I shall not know how to go on if he is badly afflicted."

"It was scarcely noticeable when I spoke to him. I daresay it only assails him when he is nervous of his audience. You must do all you can to set him at his ease."

"What are his topics of conversation?" Almeria enquired, reluctantly beginning to accept the inevitable, if daunting, prospect before her.

"It is difficult to recall, but I do know he is not enamoured of town life. He is all impatience to take up his first living in Hampshire."

"I can scarcely express too much interest in that in the circumstances, or he will think me anxious to accompany him there! It does not seem he will care for my sort of diversions like visiting the theatre and reading novels! Doubtless he regards them as twin evils and would forbid me ever to indulge in either again." She shuddered in spite of the heat.

Frances regarded her with some amusement. "You do view the opposite sex *en noir*, I must say!"

This casual observation brought forth a torrent of Merry's heart-felt views. "I have not the least intention of hurling myself at the head of the first man who offers for me—particularly if he is a clergyman who is on the catch for a helpmeet and purveyor of good works in his far-flung parish!" With growing agitation and eyes agleam she stood up and paced about. "I am not just an empty-headed female ready to succumb to the tyranny of marriage!" She fixed her cousin with an impassioned stare. "I shall want love, of course, but a respect for my mind as well as my body. But it is well-known that all gentlemen take flight at the least sign of intelligence in a girl. As Mary Wollstonecraft says in her book—"

Frances could stand no more and dissolved into laughter at this point. "For pity's sake, Merry, do stop! I *will* label you arrogant if you favour me with many more speeches of that sort. You cannot base your life on a mish-mash of contradictory notions garnered from novels of the Minerva Press and the works of Miss Wollstonecraft. As for that lady— if one can honour her with the title—I do not believe she practised what she preached for very long; and I would recommend you do not breathe her name in polite society," she added. Then, catching at her cousin's hand as she stalked past once again, said earnestly, "I have been married, you know, and I can assure you you do not need all this study and conjecture to make a favourable choice of husband. As in all such matters an ounce of mother is worth a pound of clergy—Oh, sorry! No pun intended!"

Merry was in no mood for puns, intentional or otherwise, and she drew away her hand—quite gently though, as she was aware that her cousin was trying to help, and it was still not easy for her to make any reference to her late husband. "Really, Fanny, you sound just like mama with your aphorisms! It must be infectious. But there is no comparing your situation with mine, is there?" she asked, returning to the matter in hand. "I thought you had known Captain Wren since he was a boy and long before there was any question of your marriage."

"Yes, that is so, but he wasn't the only young man of my acquaintance. However, I soon knew he was my choice."

"You were at least allowed a *choice!*"

"I believe you would have been," Frances pointed out, "if you had made the least push in the matter. After all, Cordelia and Theodosia have partners of their own choosing."

"Perhaps, but Theo has been allowed *two* seasons to become betrothed, why must I be disposed of in six months?"

"Merry, first, please have done with glaring down at me so—it is very disconcerting—and just go and sit down quietly . . . That's better. Now, I do not believe you are being 'disposed of', as you put it, but your mama feels perhaps that it will scarcely be worth chaperoning you alone next season—"

"Of course it would not," interrupted Merry. "I have not taken well *this* season—I have heard mama say so a dozen times. The shy young Denbury they call me—Theo told me!"

Frances waited for this new eruption to die away. "So," she continued patiently, "she is trying to expedite matters in her own way."

"Yes, I know, she is trying to dispose of me," reiterated Merry, "to the first person who offers for me."

Frances shook her head. "No, I suspect it may be a stratagem to jolt you out of your complacency and make you consider your future. I'm not suggesting Mr Tiffen hasn't offered for you, of course, but I very much doubt he will want an unwilling bride, so if you cried off that would be an end of it. Well, it has made you reflect on the matter already, has it not?"

"I suppose so," was the reluctant response, "and I would do almost anything to avoid another season like this one."

"—Except marry?"

Almeria smiled wanly back at her cousin. "Except marry Mr Tiffen, at all events."

"I should not dismiss Mr Tiffen so easily if I stood in your shoes." She looked thoughtfully at her cousin for a moment. "Is there no one who has taken your fancy these past months—out of all the gentlemen who have been paraded before you at routs and suppers?"

"No, none," Merry replied promptly, then hesitated. "Except for Old Harry," she murmured.

Frances's brows shot up. "Old Harry? And who is he, pray? *Not* the crossing-sweeper in the square?"

"No," giggled Merry, "of course not . . . But it would make scant difference if he were," she added, looking suddenly glum again.

"Well, you are very enigmatic," Frances commented, when it was clear no further enlightenment was forthcoming on Old Harry's identity. "But whoever he may be if it proves you have some natural feelings towards the opposite sex, it is a beginning!"

2

Frances may have regarded her cousin's feelings for Old Harry as a beginning but Almeria knew they were not: more like an end, she thought unhappily, for the object of her affections could scarcely have been more improbable or inadmissable than if she *had* cherished a tendre for a crossing-sweeper. She knew very little about the gentleman in question: had never, of course, exchanged a single word with him, and had yet to discover his real name.

That he was above her touch, she knew full well, for besides being referred to with some jocosity as Old Harry by his inmates he was on occasion addressed as Sir Harry, and his constant companion of late was apparently the son of a lord. This much she had gleaned from keeping him and his party under constant surveillance the few times she had seen him at the theatre and been within earshot. Evidently he shared with her a passion for the playhouse and the ballet; the opera she was not so sure about as their attendances at the operatic performances at the splendid King's Theatre had not so far coincided.

Her cousin did not know of Old Harry's existence because Almeria's visits to the theatre were for the most part in the company of her father alone. Cordelia was married now and lived, with her prosperous merchant husband, in Golden Square, and Theodosia had a marked preference for dancing and drawing-room pursuits rather than for the theatre, so Mrs Denbury accompanied her as chaperon with Frances as a companion for herself. Mr Denbury, as a Nabob, did not lack means and had on lease as many theatre boxes—if not more—than any member of the ton. So Drury Lane, Covent Garden, The English Opera House and the King's Theatre were all at Almeria's disposal, and except during the winter months when some theatres closed she could count on a weekly visit to one or another of them.

Almeria's first taste of the garish and exciting world of the theatre had been at Astley's Amphitheatre, where at a very early age, with her sisters, she had watched, open-mouthed, the amazing equestrian and rope-dancing acts, all presided over by the most splendid riding master in pouter-breasted military uniform. However, the display did not alter greatly with the years and she was soon petitioning her father to let her accompany him to the 'real' theatre: so, in spite of her mother's vociferous disapproval (she did not regard plays—or their audiences—as fitting spectacles for a young lady), Almeria was watching Mrs Jordan as Lady Teazle and Edmund Kean as Shylock by the time she was sixteen.

Theatre visits were not, therefore, associated in her mind in any way with her coming out, and she liked them all the more for that. The seclusion of the box and the fact that she was rarely called upon to make tongue-tied conversation with her fellows also appealed to her diffident nature. The audiences were rarely tolerant of bad performances, or even occasionally of good ones, and were often rowdy, so, in deference to Mrs Denbury's wishes they always departed before the last item of the evening, which was the farce, and also often before nine o'clock when the public were admitted at half-price.

Thus it was that she had always left the theatre with her father before Old Harry, so had no opportunity to see where he went or with whom. He was not old, of course; not above thirty, she hazarded, about the same age as Cordelia's husband. He was, she was tolerably certain, a carefree bachelor. (If not, he was a deplorable husband.) There were rarely ladies in his party and, due to this circumstance, the snatches of conversation she overheard often made her cheeks burn, and she had deduced from these that her paragon might in fact be somewhat of a rake. However, she was protected from any severe disillusionment by the hopelessness of her passion. If he were a bachelor he would be a remarkably eligible one; of that she had no doubt. He was possessed of a dark patrician countenance and a most perturbing smile: his dress, of constant variety, bespoke wealth and the best tailor—and she was sure *he* was a good deal more than five-feet-nine.

It was hardly to be expected, therefore, that Mr Jonathan Tiffen could hope to match such a formidable rival. The fact that Old Harry was a rival only in the mind of Almeria made little difference to the result: she inevitably compared the few gentlemen of her acquaintance to her idol and they were all found to be sadly wanting.

She knew what the eminently sensible Fanny would say to all this if she knew: that it was mere youthful infatuation, and Old Harry little more than an extension of the play-acting on the stage. And Fanny would be right, of course, but Almeria was not going to abandon her dreams yet awhile: not for the likes of Mr Tiffen, in any event.

Such thoughts were not ideal ones to be having as she dressed for dinner on that fateful Friday, but Almeria was doing her utmost to ignore the coming ordeal and concentrate on the following week when the whole family, including Cordelia, were going to the theatre. Covent Garden was staging *Romeo and Juliet*.

She was trying to decide between a gown of blue French spotted silk, which she liked but was cut very low at the bosom, and one with a white silk skirt and primrose satin bodice, a trifle more demure but insipid, when her sister, Theodosia, burst forth into the bedchamber.

"May I come in, Merry?" she enquired belatedly, although that she asked at all was an innovation. The reason for this cursory respect was soon forthcoming. "Mama has this minute told me your amazing news! How have you managed to keep it to yourself for so long? But you were always a dark one." She stood beside Almeria, who was holding at arm's length the demure dress, and although the sisters were of a height Almeria felt at once that she faded into insignificance. Theo was already dressed for the evening in pink gauze over crimson satin—colours which Merry was content to leave to the fashion plates in the *Lady's Magazine*. "Oh yes, that reminds me, mama asked me to send Travers in to you tonight when she had dressed me—she will be here at any moment."

"There's no call for that. I always dress myself," Almeria murmured. She was upset that Mr Tiffen's offer had been made known to Theo: this would serve to increase her apprehensions if she felt everyone's eyes upon them at dinner.

"Well, tonight is rather special, surely? Although how you contrived to ensnare your clergyman I cannot imagine. If you knew how I *toiled* to fix Plumptree's interest—it was the work of weeks. Tiffen has always looked so *inanimate*," she added in a wondering voice. Before her sister had time to deny the charge of ensnaring, Theo continued impatiently: "Which one are you going to wear, then? I would favour the primrose, you know: there could be nothing in that to revolt the most delicate religious sensibilities, could there? And it must be your quiet, modest air which attracts, I suppose . . ." She looked at her young sister, and was obviously at a complete stand that anyone should have offered for her, for any reason, but her comments decided Almeria.

"No, I shall wear the spotted silk," she said with determination, hoping it *would* be sufficient to outrage the most delicate religious sensibilities. She snatched it up wishing she could borrow one of Theo's more daring gowns but it would need to be taken in at least two inches, and there was no time.

"I think you may be making a mistake," observed Theo. "Ah, here's Travers now."

"The mistress needs my services as well tonight, Miss Almeria, so if it please you I should be glad if we can start right away," the lady's maid said.

"Of course, Travers." She turned to her sister

rather diffidently. "Perhaps you had better leave us, or I shall only squander time in gossip."

Theo, already piqued at having her advice scorned, looked mildly surprised at this unwonted dismissal, but said, "Oh, very well, if you don't want the benefit of my experience—it is of complete indifference to me."

Without her colourful presence to overshadow her, Almeria tried to visualize herself more extravagantly adorned: she would try to repel Mr Tiffen, it was the only device she could think of at the eleventh hour. It would awaken the wrath of her mother, but that was never difficult and would be a small price to pay for Mr Tiffen's departure from the scene.

As Travers was in haste to attend Mrs Denbury, Almeria had little difficulty in dismissing her as soon as she was dressed and her hair braided. Her aim was simple—to look as much like the painted minxes she had seen in the theatre pit as she dared— but the means were far from easy. She had no carmine or rouge, or even burnt cork to darken her fair eyebrows. However, Fanny had told her repeatedly —when she had wanted to improve her complexion —that the use of paint was a sign of bad breeding, and the *careless* use of it placed one beyond the pale; so, every embellishment would be bound to have a startling impact, she assumed. She set to work on her cheeks with a dampened scarlet ribbon. Cork, to burn in a candle, she could not procure at such short

notice, and she wished she had paid more attention
to the ingenious hints sometimes given in the maga-
zines. As she scrubbed away at her cheeks she considered soot from the chimney but decided against
that: she did not want to look like a clown from
Astley's Amphitheatre.

She removed the pearls, which were customary
for a young lady, and searched her jewellery box
for something more dazzling; coral, amber or garnets were her only choice. The garnets were not
exactly dazzling but were the showiest jewellery she
possessed. So, the matching ear-rings, necklace,
and a bracelet which slipped over her elbow-length
gloves of white kid, completed her ensemble. But
then her eye was caught by the gold watch on a
chain, which could hang from her high-waisted
dress, and she added that with a final defiant gesture.

The bell sounded, warning the family the dinner
guests would be due at any moment, and Almeria
leapt up as if it were a pistol shot. All her apprehensions returned, and she had never felt less like eating
a dinner. Luckily, she was at home and if she left
her food it could not be counted a reproach to her
hostess: as for her mother's unfavourable reaction
that would be certain in any event now. She did
not dare look in the mirror again in case her resolve
should waver, and snatching up her fan she went
towards the door. It then occurred to her that if she
were too early upon the scene her mother would

send her away to wash her face and remove the offending jewellery, so she stayed where she was for a time, shivering in the warm bedchamber. Her cousin's arrival curtailed the delay almost at once.

"Merry, your mama is asking for you in the drawing-room," Frances said as she put her head round the door.

"Yes, I was just this moment ready," Almeria replied, turning away from the door as if to collect something from the dressing-table. "Do go on ahead, I am coming, I promise." She must keep her face shielded from Fanny for as long as possible . . . Experiencing the awful tremors of apprehension which always assailed her before meeting company, but of even greater intensity on this occasion, she followed Frances, who turned to look at her five yards from the drawing-room doors. Almeria unfurled her fan, which was distressingly small, and hid her blushes behind it.

"Oh, I'm so glad you've chosen the blue—it suits your colouring so well," Frances said, without evidently noticing the latter's transformation. "Mr Tiffen is here already," she added.

This shattering intelligence put to flight all thought of her complexion as Almeria advanced into the room—but not with her usual reluctant caution. For it was her intention to be as bold as she had been shy, and as brazen as she had been modest, to accord with her shameless appearance and to put the unwelcome suitor to flight.

Her parents and both her sisters were there with Cordelia's merchant husband, Mr Charles Vine, and Mr Tiffen, whom she soon saw with her father by the great sphinx-framed mirror.

"Oh, Almeria, there you are, my love," cried her mother with quite as much artificiality in her voice as Almeria could hope to produce.

She was swept towards Mr Tiffen and found herself blinking at a pleasant-faced young man, smiling uncertainly. What kind eyes, she thought, and automatically tried to set him at his ease: that he was nervous was quite plain.

"M—m—miss—"

"Oh, do, I beg you, call me Almeria," she cut in; his stammer, which she had quite forgotten, disconcerting her further. But then, recalling her saucy role, she smiled as impudently as she knew how.

It seemed though that he was reassured by this, for he replied without the least hesitation to his speech. "Thank you. And I am Jonathan—it will be so much more comfortable if we can be on the easiest of terms from the beginning, will it not?" Then he went on to say, quite as smoothly: "Your father has just been telling me what devotees you both are of the theatre."

"Oh yes, indeed—I expect you must disapprove greatly of such a taste," she said hopefully.

"Not the least in the world! In fact I was expressing my admiration for Mr Shakespeare's plays to your father only a moment ago, and he has most kindly invited me to accompany the family next week to see *Romeo and Juliet*. I expect you must have seen it before but I confess it will be a novelty to me."

This reply dealt a double blow to Almeria: she had been counting on his disapprobation of her relish for the theatre, and it had never occurred to her that he would be invited to be one of their party the following week.

"Oh no, I have not seen that play," she said, recovering herself. "I must own," she went on, intent once again upon being as reprehensible as could be, "I have a preference for Mr Sheridan's works—*A School for Scandal* is a particular favourite of mine."

Mr Tiffen shook his head sadly, raising hope in his hearer's breast that she had succeeded at last in shocking him. "Poor Sheridan! It is a grievous thing to see a man of his talents drinking himself into a decline," was all he said, though.

Almeria thought she might be the recipient of a sermon on the evil of drink but instead her companion embarked on a dissertation on the remarkable genius of Mr Kemble and his sister, Mrs Siddons, in Shakespearian parts: in spite of herself she was drawn into a discussion. From this she discovered that Mr Tiffen (she could not really think of him as Jonathan) had been in town for the past two seasons, lodged with the uncle from whom he derived his expectations.

As the conversation veered towards the personal, and in particular to the living in Hampshire, which awaited Mr Tiffen, Almeria was relieved when Theodosia approached them. "Really, Merry, you are quite monopolizing Mr Tiffen! Look to the other guests, I wish Mr Tiffen to make the acquaintance of my Mr Plumptree, who has this minute arrived."

Almeria was glad, of course, to be released from the conversation as it was approaching delicate ground, but her innate shyness quickly engulfed her when faced with the prospect of intruding upon one of the chattering groups about her. Thankfully, she caught Fanny's eye just as an unknown gentleman was leaving her cousin: she went over to her.

"My word, you do look flushed," Frances greeted her, causing Almeria to fan herself with sudden violence, as she had quite forgotten her blowzy appearance. "I trust you haven't contracted the fever, Merry. Are you feeling quite well?"

"Perfectly, thank you," she answered stiffly.

Frances still regarded her a little doubtfully, but observed, "You and Mr Tiffen seem to be dealing very well together! What did I tell you? I knew you would find him most refined in manner."

"I suppose he is," agreed Almeria, pausing in her fanning to look across the Egyptian salon at that gentleman: he had an air of breeding, and although he had not yet assumed the gaitered garb of the clergy he affected a style of dress which was

all that one could wish, even if a trifle sombre for
her own taste. Certainly her father's description,
although without doubt evocative, was comparable
in accuracy to a Cruikshank caricature of the
Prince Regent—whom she had seen once at the
theatre. Mr Tiffen's eyes *were* a trifle close but
were in themselves amiable and attractive, which
was more important. The rest of his face had a
tendency to plumpness and his hair, though almost
as dark as Old Harry's, complemented a much
fresher complexion than his. "He likes the theatre,
it seems," she added gloomily.

"There you are! You were much too morose in
your estimation of the poor man."

So swiftly had the time passed that dinner was
announced at that moment and Almeria found
herself once again at Mr Tiffen's side, being led
into the dining-room. She was seated between him
and Theo's affianced, George Plumptree, whom
she knew scarcely better than Mr Tiffen. Consequently, she turned to talk almost exclusively to
the gentleman of her parents' choice—as it was intended she should.

"You are fond of country life, M—m—" He
gave a quick nervous smile. "Almeria?"

"Oh no, I could not in all honesty say that,"
she protested with great firmness, determined once
again to display a disposition quite unsuited to a
clergyman's wife. "I am much too attached to the
pleasures of the town," she said brightly, hoping

it sounded as dissolute to his ears as it did to her own.

"Well, that is very natural: you are young. I'm sure I should not expect—that is," he amended hastily, "when I go into Hampshire I do not intend to cut my connexion with town life entirely. I have kinsmen and acquaintance here whom I would be loth to abandon. But, after all, 'God made the country, and man made the town,' as Mr Cowper so rightly observed, and I believe the town life will pall on you in time."

Almeria saw an opportunity here to turn the subject to more neutral ground, and her vast reading stood her in good stead. "Oh, you have read 'The Task', have you? I do so admire Mr Cowper's verses."

And so did Mr Tiffen, apparently, and the subject lasted them through another course: and after that conversation became general around the table due to her father's retailing of the rumours he had heard flying about the city that day.

"But I thought the Stock Exchange was closed today," Mr Plumptree remarked, somewhat diffidently, to his future father-in-law.

"So it is, my boy," concurred Mr Denbury, in his expansive way, "which renders the rumours all the more powerful in my view. The whole of the south of France is said to be in a turmoil because it is confidently expected a division of the Toulon Fleet intends to intercept the ship, *Northumber-*

land, and bring Bonaparte back to France to start his tricks again."

"But didn't we defeat him, or something, at Waterloo, papa?" put in Cordelia, with a puzzled frown: her grasp of public affairs was not of a powerful order.

"Of course we did," her father responded, a shade less expansively this time. "The fellow set sail in the *Northumberland* on the eighth of this month from Torbay for exile in St. Helena. *Now* there is talk of yet another escape, and it has thrown the 'Change into a dreadful pucker."

"I wouldn't trust that odious man an inch even if he is in the middle of the Atlantic Ocean," declared his wife. "There's no smoke without some fire, where he's concerned."

The general apprehension engendered by the thought of Bonaparte's return, and more conflict on the scale of the recent dreadful battle at Waterloo, spread about the table and continued unabated until Mrs Denbury led away the ladies, leaving her husband deep in conversation with his merchant son-in-law, Charles Vine, about the state of their imperilled investments. Mr Plumptree talked to Mr Tiffen of the matter in more general terms, neither being possessed of threatened stocks.

Almeria had dreaded the close scrutiny of the ladies, whilst the gentlemen's arrival in the drawing-room was awaited, but to her surprise no one took particular note of her; not even to torment her about Mr Tiffen. She had quite thought her mother would single her out before the company because of her tawdry looks.

When the gentlemen did return, the tea tray was brought in, and whist being one of the Denbury vices it was not long before two tables were made up. There were twelve guests in all so four were spectators. Almeria was still bent on proving her depravity so for once she eagerly partnered her stolid brother-in-law, Mr Vine. Cordelia, his wife, found whist quite beyond her powers of concentration and she joined Frances, Mr Tiffen and another gentleman as observers.

Consequently, although Almeria had to be present until the bitter end of the evening's entertainment she had little more private conversation with Mr Tiffen. At last every guest had departed, and her head really did ache abominably now, but she braced herself for the inevitable scolding from her mother before she could seek the refuge of her bed.

There was no delay: Mrs Denbury bore down on her young daughter even as the butler bore down on the debris in the drawing-room. "Almeria, pray don't rush away, my dear, although I'm sure you must be quite exhausted."

Oh dear, thought Almeria, she is at her most sarcastic . . .

"You were in such glowing good looks tonight. I cannot recall when you have looked so—so radiant. And such an effort you have made with your appearance—so gratifying! The watch was perhaps just a little de trop . . . but no matter, you look splendid. I knew you would see the sense in complying with our wishes, and Mr Tiffen was quite enchanted with you—anyone could see that! And how you did chatter! Well, with things moving apace like this we shall have you engaged quicker than a Hounslow horse-change. Now, you trip along to your bed, my dear." Then, as a final astonishment in an astonishing speech, she concluded, "You may have a breakfast tray in your room in the morning."

3

Almeria was unfortunately in no mood to enjoy the rare luxury of breakfast in bed, the morning after her unlooked-for success at the first conscious meeting with Jonathan Tiffen. Still smarting under the irony of a situation which had established her as a complaisant girl trying to charm her future husband, instead of a hussy bent on scandalizing all about her, Almeria had slept but little. A night of restless cogitation, however, had not produced a scheme to extricate her from her present impasse. She appeared to be left only with the petulant resolve of every young schoolroom martyr—

to run away. But, like the schoolroom miss, she had precious little hope of realising the aim. Her refuge would have to be far-flung, welcoming, and also unlikely to be discovered by her parents. As her only distant—and possibly sympathetic—country connexion was her maternal grandmother in Devonshire, whom she had never even visited but who had stayed several times at Bedford Square, the outlook was not hopeful. She lacked money, knowledge of coach travel (beyond a realisation that she would be a rather conspicuous traveller by reason of her youth and her sex) and, above all, she lacked the courage to attempt such a hazardous operation. She had read numberless tales of highwaymen on Hounslow Heath, overturned coaches, and passengers frozen to death—not, it is true, in August but who could tell when she might have to leave?

Being bookish she had naturally considered going for a governess, as heroines of novels so often did, but she knew the limitations of her own character too well to take that course: she would quickly be put to rout by the first obstreperous young charge she encountered. Besides, her musical accomplishments were limited: her innate timidity had always precluded any drawing-room performance and consequently her tuition had been of the most rudimentary nature. The other course open to her was as companion to some decrepit old lady, probably resident in one of the spas; there were frequent advertisements in the newspapers for such posts. But Fanny had rejected that alternative for herself when she had been widowed, and had often discussed the miseries she had avoided by doing so.

In theory, Mary Wollstonecraft's ideas about being independent of men were all very well, Almeria thought, and made a natural appeal to one trying to avoid an arranged marriage, but the reality was different, as she was discovering. If she were honest, not a great deal of *A Vindication of the Rights of Woman* had been understood by her, but the general rebellious theme had struck a sympathetic chord. She sighed, and a feeling of great languor came over her as she set the tray aside and gave up trying to partake of any breakfast. Then, slowly, an idea did come to her . . .

It would require a degree of dissembling, but not of the same order of acting she had had to attempt at the dinner-party. Yes, that was it, she would feign illness—nothing specific, perhaps a malaise of the spirits accompanied by a spasmodic hollow cough which could convince those about her she was sinking into a confirmed consumption. It should not be too difficult: her mother had always regarded her as the sickly one of the family because of her fair complexion and studious ways. Still, it must be finely judged. She had no desire to be bed-ridden for the rest of her days, or even house-bound. A thought struck her which momentarily weakened her resolve; she would have to forego her theatre visits and, therefore, all opportunity of seeing Old Harry. But a moment's further reflection told her that marriage to Mr Tiffen would have exactly the same effect, with a host of permanent disadvantages besides.

No, her scheme was definitely to be preferred. Once Mr Tiffen had been persuaded she was quite unequal to the rigours of matrimony and child-bearing, she could stage a gradual recovery and eventually resume her present mode of life. She felt sure he would discover a successor for her in no time at all believing, as she did, that his affections were not seriously engaged on this occasion. However, if he did not turn his attentions elsewhere, the timing of her improvement would be a matter for the finest judgement—but she must leave that to future decision. Old Harry might have quit the scene by then, but it was a risk she had to take; and anyway, at heart, she knew that any sanguine expectation in that direction to be a romantical high-flight; he would never, in a lifetime of play-going, even notice her and, if he did, she would be as tongue-tied and stupid as ever!

Having made her decision she felt vastly better, drew back the tray, and had eaten two pieces of French bread and honey before she realised her appetite had best be a little impaired from now on . . .

In the event, she postponed the beginning of her

decline until after the family visit to *Romeo and Juliet*. It would definitely be her last excursion into the world for many a long day, and it might just afford her a final look at Old Harry to sustain her through her impending ordeal.

Mrs Denbury, still, it seemed, in perfect charity with her youngest daughter, offered to buy her a new dress for the coming occasion. "—For I realised when I saw you on Friday," she told Almeria, "that with just the least effort on your part— which hitherto has been conspicuously lacking, I may say—you can look quite presentable. I would suggest you choose something a trifle gayer than your usual taste." Although more benevolent, Mrs Denbury did not take her new-found interest in Almeria too far: she did not accompany her to buy the dress.

Instead Frances went with her cousin, and they set out a couple of days before the theatre visit for what turned out to be an orgy of shopping. Selecting the dress had been no problem for Almeria: she fell in love at once with a quite dazzling gown, with a skirt of silver lamé over gauze and three tiers of mulberry velvet flouncing round the hem— the somewhat scanty bodice and tiny puffed sleeves were also a rich mulberry. Even in the subdued daylight of the shop the skirt shimmered amazingly, and at the bright candelit theatre Almeria thought it would look the dashiest thing imaginable. Her motives for buying such a dress were confused, to say the least: she was still intent upon shocking

Mr Tiffen as much as possible just in case her
other scheme faltered, and although she would
scarcely admit it to herself she did just hope a
really brilliant dress would perhaps attract the attention of one particular gentleman. However,
drawing notice upon herself was not in her nature
and she knew really that the other occupants of
the boxes would outshine her every time.

"Do you really think that is quite the thing at
your age?" demanded Frances. "It is a little—well,
actressy, I fear."

Splendid! thought Almeria. "Mama was most
particular I should select something bright, so I
have."

"Yes, well, there's bright and then there's *that,*"
Frances responded, indicating the glittering lamé.
"Now, what about the pink satin with the van-
dyked flounces—I think it most charming."

However, at this critical point, the proprietress
of the exclusive establishment gave her opinion that
the silver lamé was *enchanté,* and it would be a
crime to choose anything else for the young lady:
it was, of course, much more expensive than the
pink satin.

Frances capitulated as she was in no way a
guardian of her cousin, nor of her Uncle Denbury's purse-strings. However, by the time Merry
had conducted her through the portals of the
mercer's, the milliner's, the haberdasher's, and then
finally to Layton and Shear, the linen draper's, she
felt moved to protest at this lavish expenditure as

they waited to be served. "I cannot understand it, Merry. One would suppose you were stocking up for a siege! Gloves and stockings by the dozen, ribbon, two morning-dresses—quite the prettiest I have seen, it is true—and now materials. Why, usually you take but scant interest in clothes-buying and make haste to the bookseller's at the first possible moment."

"Well, yes," responded Almeria, seizing upon the last remark, "that is it, I suppose. I realise my wardrobe has sunk alarmingly low."

Frances looked a trifle sceptical. "I quite thought you must have decided to impress Mr Tiffen. I own to being wholly puzzled at your attitude towards him since Friday, but, nonetheless I fancy you are stocking up against a life in the Hampshire countryside, are you not?" she concluded mischievously.

Almeria tried to calculate if it would be more convincing to her plan if Fanny thought she had been considering accepting Mr Tiffen's offer when she was struck down by illness. She was saved any answer, though, when the draper's assistant approached at that moment. Consequently, she kept her counsel and, by the time they went to Covent Garden, Frances felt almost certain that Almeria meant to accept Jonathan Tiffen. It was not in Merry's nature to deceive anyone, least of all Frances who was such a good friend, but she could not jeopardize her scheme—not even for her.

Merry had bought a new supply of scarlet ribbon, suspecting that her original one had not yielded the depth of blush to her cheeks she had thought it would. She looked more closely at the results of her handiwork this time and was quite pleased with her glowing looks as she put on the garnets once more. Her mother had seen the lamé dress when Almeria had brought it home and had expressed no qualms about it: it accorded well with her own taste for the bright and exotic. Her particular choice for the evening was puce satin with orange trimmings.

The Denbury carriage was full to over-flowing when the party left for the theatre. Mr and Mrs Denbury and Jonathan Tiffen were seated on one side: Theo, Almeria and Frances were on the other. Merry was sitting bodkin and for once was not outshone by her sisters: this time Fanny looked the pale, modestly-dressed one of the trio. Mr Tiffen gave Almeria a slight smile occasionally, but conversation was difficult across the carriage due to the noise of the wheels. His smiles were absent-mindedly returned by Merry but her thoughts were wholly upon what was probably her last night out for months to come, and whether or not Old Harry was also at this moment making his way to Covent Garden Theatre.

Captain Sir Henry Cedric Jasper Chirton, Bt, sat in his usual place by the hearth at *Tom's* coffee house in Russell-street waiting for his friend to arrive. A coffee house was a trifle bourgeois, he knew, as a meeting place but he had fallen into the habit

of frequenting these convivial establishments when
alone. But tonight, in spite of the usual bustle and
noise of the customers, it depressed him; he stared
at the empty summer grate and was further cast
down.

The cause of his gloom had no particular root.
Today was much like any other day for him: a
leisurely rising, the latter part of the morning spent
calling upon various acquaintances: in the afternoon, visits to the tailor, bootmaker or Tattersall's
(the high-change of horse-flesh, as it was called),
with perhaps an hour or so at Gentleman John
Jackson's Pugilistic Club—for he was anxious that
the foot injury he had sustained during his time in
the Peninsula should not be allowed to impair his
boxing skill more than was unavoidable: then,
when the evening started, he invariably sought the
company of Major the Hon. Crispin Maunby, who
had made a triumphant return from the battlefield
of Waterloo—and from that moment, the previous
month, there was no shortage of entertainment or
high spirits, for Crispin had an irrespressibly cheerful disposition which even Bonaparte's worst efforts
had failed to crush. As Crispin was seven-and-
twenty and he himself was nearing thirty, their noc-
turnal escapades were not quite the riotous capers
that, seven or eight years before, had landed them
in Bow-street. Since that time they had both seen
enough of real battles to have much relish for

starting a mill with their foxed fellows at a badger-baiting or cock-fight.

There was nothing unusual in this daily routine for a gentleman of means and leisure, particularly one with neither dependents nor responsibilities as Sir Henry was. For some time after he had had to sell out his commission at the early age of six-and-twenty, due to his being wounded, he had chafed against retiring to this sort of town life. But gradually he accepted it and, when the victory at Waterloo saw the return of his good companion of earlier army days, he had been much relieved and inspirited. Indeed, for the past few weeks Crispin and he had had an uproarious time together, but now he felt blue-devilled . . .

"Well, aren't you going to speak to me, you grim-gilled old varmint?" Crispin demanded. "From your woebegone expression I'd hazard there's a fastener out for you at the very least of it, and you stare Newgate in the face!"

His friend jerked up his head and at once a welcoming smile put flight to his gloomy looks. "Crispin! No, of course there isn't! I don't play deep, you know that, and I haven't quite frittered away my inheritance as yet, although the past few weeks' frolics have made a sizeable dent in it, I fancy!"

This careless, light-hearted response rendered Crispin sober for once and his fair, almost school-boyish face looked momentarily solemn. As a younger son he was wholly dependent upon the whims of his father for his allowance and had no expectations whatever—until he married, an event he had not the slightest wish to precipitate. "Yes, such a monstrous drain on my own resources has not escaped notice, I can tell you." He sank down in a battered wooden chair the other side of the dead grate, and signalled to the serving-man.

His friend apologised. "I'm sorry, old fellow, but you introduced the vexed matter of blunt. I should have been despondent, of course, if those rumours of Boney's escape back to France had turned out true—my fortune would have dwindled overnight, along with many others."

Crispin ordered coffee, then called after the servant: "No, make that a cognac." Turning to his friend, he added, "Just as well I can still afford something stronger than coffee. I need it after a few minutes of your heartening company!" He sighed gustily. "You know nothing would suit *me* better than to see Boney back again. I wouldn't be kicking my heels on half-pay, and there might be a chance then of being lieutenant-colonel by the time I was thirty."

"By George, you're a real fire-eater these days! Aren't you satisfied that you have outstripped your old comrade-in-arms, who achieved a mere captaincy? Just be grateful you didn't leave a limb behind in the Belgian mud, and have done with the fighting." He knew full well how he felt, though: he had suffered the same frustrations after his last battle at Salamanca.

"I am grateful, of course, when I think of the state some poor devils are in." Crispin accepted the brandy from the man, an ineffable expression on his face for a moment. But he soon made an attempt to banish his grim reflections, and said in a voice more like his usual jaunty manner: "You know what the alternative prospect is for me—marriage!"

"A splendid institution," remarked Sir Henry blandly.

"That comes well from you, I must say," spluttered Crispin, "the town's most inveterate bachelor—despaired of by every mama! Besides," he added sardonically, "you are not expected to get leg-shackled to Meg Venables!"

"Oh, very true, but then I had no idea it was expected of you either!"

"Well, it is. M'mother's got it into her noodle that we're made for each other. They're just waiting for me to sell-out, and then play the country squire at Whitemead."

"Really!" exclaimed Sir Henry. "I had no idea such a sword of Damocles hung over you—you seemed so sunny of late."

"I am blessed with a naturally optimistic nature—besides, I was perfectly sure Boney could be relied upon to escape just once more!"

"Well, I suspect you are glaringly abroad there: he'll not get up to any more of his tricks in St. Helena."

"But he's not there yet," protested Crispin.

"I can't see him slipping from Admiral Cockburn's grasp at this stage, even if the whole French fleet challenges him—which I would deem very unlikely." He leaned back in his chair and crossed his legs. "No, I think you'd better tell me about Miss Venables."

An appalled expression passed over Crispin's features, at odds with his glowing healthy looks.

"As bad as that, eh? Let me guess what the lady is like, shall I, if you can't bear to dwell on the subject . . . Past five-and-twenty, I collect?"

"Almost one-and-twenty," murmured his friend.

"Oh . . . well, then, she must be a sallow, angular maypole of a girl, a stride like a sentry and a voice like a sergeant-major . . . oh yes, and with a deplorable taste in clothes, and a—a passion for eating cabbage," he concluded triumphantly. "No! pray don't laugh—it was the latter failing, you must know, which damped Brummell's ardour on one famous occasion."

"Oh, Harry!" Crispin gasped, his customary good humour restored once more. "I don't think even my parent would wish such a harridan on me, be she as rich as Croesus!"

"Which this young lady must be, I fancy? When you have caught your breath you had best enlighten me. I can see I haven't quite hit the mark in every detail."

Crispin shook his head. "I hardly know how to, to tell the truth. I haven't seen her above two or three times— I have, as you know, been from home rather a lot in past years. The last time was a twelve-month ago when the proposal was first put to me. Even then, she had settled both my fate and Whitemead's to her own satisfaction for the next decade." He shuddered. "I can't abide managing women, however prettily they look."

"There is nothing decided, is there?" asked Sir Henry, worried, not liking the sound of this. "No understanding which it would be difficult to escape honourably?"

"Good God, no! I left all parties in no doubt that I was wedded to the regiment. But now I am not so firmly wedded, I'm damned if I dare set foot on the ancestral acres for fear of being abducted! That's why I took the coward's way out and postponed going into Berkshire until the season was over in town. But that's not going to fadge much longer—in August!"

"Well, as I see it you have only one alternative. Find a wife of your own choosing—unless, of course, your father can withhold whatever monies are due to you on marriage if he does not approve of the lady?"

"Oh no! It is not of his ordering: a favourite aunt —God bless her—bequeathed the money, with marriage as a pre-condition. Meg Venables just happens to be a considerable heiress—for a younger son, in any event," he said with some acerbity. "But I refuse to be tied to a virago, however rich."

"Quite right—a terrible fate for any man. So—what of my solution? You are dashing, gay, not un-handsome, of modest fortune—even something of a hero—with the outside chance of an earldom. It shouldn't be difficult to place you."

"I am much obliged to you for the character reference," Crispin said wryly, "but I am not a housemaid of yours—thank heaven! If you are setting up the Chirton marriage mart you may begin with yourself, not me! It is rich, is it not," he continued, his indignation growing, "that you with your comfortable bachelor life and your *chère amie*, should throw me, your old friend, to the wolves."

Sir Henry took this castigation without a blink, and said placatingly: "I am merely trying to help in what appears to me a parlous situation. I take it that your circumstances would benefit from the infusion of money on your marriage?"

"Dammit, of course it would!" he cried, his colour rising. "Oh, I'm not exactly at point-non-plus, but I can't continue in this style for ever."

"Exactly so," murmured Sir Henry, feeling a trifle guilty about his own comfortable circumstances which had perhaps indirectly led his friend into greater expense than he could support.

"—Anyway," Crispin went on, "I thought we set out to discuss *your* fit of the sullens not mine!"

"Oh, that was of no account, just a temporary ennui—nothing I could lay a finger on, precisely.

But that is quite dispersed—I have an occupation henceforth."

Crispin was executing a weary but comprehensive arm-stretch that put the seams of his close-fitting coat at considerable risk, but he stopped abruptly. "Occupation?" he echoed suspiciously.

"Oh, a very pleasant one—I regard it in no way as an imposition. I shall enjoy finding a wife for you."

"Now look here, Harry, I can manage that for myself—"

"But demonstrably, you can't! You're falling into a quite pitiful pucker over La Venables. You need help and help you shall have. We'll start tonight."

"Tonight?" Crispin said faintly, his jauntiness deserting him. "We're not promised to old Lady Teign's tonight, are we?"

"Certainly not! As if I should expose you to the sort of middle-aged, dragonish maidens you would encounter there. No, we shall be adventurous—tread new paths, search fresh coverts—"

"I thought we might look in at Watier's," Crispin suggested, ignoring these rustic exhortations. "I must be due for a run of luck at the tables."

"No females there," said Sir Henry briskly. "Besides you can't afford a run of the sort of luck you'd most likely get. I suggest the theatre—we're only a step away from either Old Drury or the Garden."

Crispin stared. "You don't propose I should wed an actress! Just because you've taken an Italian dancer for a mistress—delightful though she may be —don't mean I—"

"No, of course, it don't," his companion said soothingly. "I meant we should scrutinize the boxes—there are some choice wares on display there at times, and from my frequenting of the playhouse I shall most likely know who they are— and if I don't, it will be no puzzle to find out."

"It sounds as buffle-headed a way to find a wife as ever I've heard! You've run mad, Harry."

"Maybe," he grinned, "but it has a touch of originality, don't you agree? What is there to lose?" His hearer looked as though he was about to tell him, so he continued hastily, "If there is nothing to your taste we shall leave as soon as you say."

"I cannot abide one more dull dramatic piece at Drury Lane, not if—if Nell Gwynn is in the *same* box!" he declared with feeling.

"You pitch it a little strong, perhaps, but I do agree. The London theatre is in the doldrums at present, there is no denying that. I suggest Covent Garden—they are presenting *Romeo and Juliet*, I fancy, and that should provide a background of high romantic fervour—very apt."

"Come, Harry, you've had your jest. You cannot be serious about all this."

"But of course I am! Pluck up—who knows where this might lead us? Where's your spirit of adventure, man?"

This appeal had Crispin on the point of surren-

der, when a brief gleam of hope came into his eye.
"You have a pressing engagement at the Argyle
Rooms tonight, surely?"

"Tomorrow," came the smug response. "Well,"
continued Sir Henry, getting to his feet, "let us be
on our way. The one-act play will be almost done,
and the interval before the main piece will provide
valuable time for reconnoitering."

In the event, the performance had made a late
start and they missed scarcely a word of the preliminary play.

"I shall repair to the Saloon downstairs for refreshment if that gentleman declaims for much
longer," groaned Crispin, *sotto voce,* once they were
settled in Sir Henry's box.

"Please, patience! Do not regard him—no one
else appears to be doing so!" He put up his glass
and turned his attention to the occupants of the
curved tiers of boxes. His own had a good vantage
point and he could discern most of the occupied
ones.

"The place is half-empty," observed Crispin. "No
one who is anybody will be here tonight, that is
obvious," he added crushingly.

"We are, are we not, so it does not follow."

"Only because of your wild goose chase!"

"Swan, my dear fellow—Ah, and if I'm not
mistaken there is one, now. Just to the left there,
by that cluster of lights. See what you think," he
whispered.

Crispin took a brief, irritated look. "Really, Harry, she looks like an over-stuffed bolster! And I don't altogether care for that lusty giant at her side. Are you trying to arrange an untimely end for me?"

"Well, if you won't search for yourself, how am I to know what your paragon might look like?"

"Not remotely like that, in any event," said Crispin shortly, and joined in the scrutiny in spite of his resolve not to.

"Now, there's a positive swoop of swans, or whatever they're called. Careful, they're just to our left."

"Mm." Crispin sounded non-committal as he followed his friend's gaze with an opera-glass.

"Well?"

He decided to humour his friend: it seemed the only way. "Yes, I can see three very presentable ladies—probably with their parents and a youngish man. So?"

"So, there may be three, or at worst, two unattached maidens for you to choose from."

Crispin gave a sudden laugh. "This is a shatter-brained scheme, Harry, even for us!"

Sir Henry noticed his friend had said 'us' and not 'you', which sounded hopeful. "But they are a remarkable attractive bevy of beauties, you must admit. Come, there must be one which engages your interest?"

"Perhaps—but, dash it, they could be *anybody!* It's a blind bargain if ever there was one."

"They look to be persons of some distinction to me—and you wanted a game of chance tonight, did you not? I have it! I'll wager you a thousand pounds I shall have found you a wife by the end of the year!"

"Now I *know* your senses are disordered! I had rather have the thousand pounds than a chance-met wife—who would not?"

"I dare swear you would," Henry laughed softly, "but if you accept the wager you must at least allow me to put one or two candidates in your way."

"You're incorrigible," groaned Crispin. "You know full well I could never resist a bet, but this one is a gift! Very well . . . But Harry—nothing that goes beyond the bounds of what is seemly. I'll not have innocent maidens put to the blush by your crack-skull notions."

"You wrong me! The affair shall be handled with the utmost delicacy and respect for all concerned."

Crispin eyed him dubiously nonetheless. "So, what do you propose I do in this particular instance—knock on the door of their box and enquire if there are any marriageable ladies in the party?"

"Well, that would have a certain *élan,* it is true, but I think we will be a shade more subtle in our approach. Leave it to me," said Harry, as the actor ceased his declaiming at last.

4

The Denbury carriage drew up at the recently re-built Covent Garden Theatre, and the four pillars of the small portico shone blindingly in the late sunlight as they went in. It was some minutes before Almeria's eyes became accustomed to the comparatively dim lighting of the auditorium, but she could see well enough her sister, Theo's, discontented features: a message had been left at the theatre office from her betrothed, George Plumptree, sending his regrets but he feared horse distemper had been detected in his stables and felt obliged to stay home.

"It is gratifying, I do declare, to know one comes

62

second in esteem to a quadruped," Theo complained as they settled themselves in their places. "No, thank you, sir," she said to Mr Tiffen's offer of a seat near the front of the box. "I'm sure I don't care if I see the stupid play or not."

A churlish remark of this sort from Almeria would have incurred immediate censure from their mother, but now Mrs Denbury merely patted the seat beside her and invited Theo to take it. "You may see all that is necessary of the stage from here, and yet be shielded from the vulgar gaze of the rabble."

Mr Denbury, as a matter of courtesy, also took a seat nearer the back leaving Almeria, Frances, and Jonathan Tiffen at the front. Their box was in the second tier of the horseshoe-shaped hall, away to the left of the stage. As soon as her vision improved Almeria took a hasty look to her right, where she knew Old Harry's box to be: Mr Tiffen was seated immediately at her left with all the other members of their party so she hoped to be able to observe this, to her, focal point of the theatre while everyone else's attention was on the stage. For the moment, however, her contriving was wasted; the box was deserted. Ridiculously she felt as let down as Theo.

"All the gilding and decoration is quite m-m-magnificent, is it not?" remarked Mr Tiffen to Almeria, making her start with guilt: she had quite forgotten his existence.

"Oh yes, indeed it is. You must have known the old theatre that was burned down, I collect?"

He shook his head. "That was back in the year eight, wasn't it, and I was a mere stripling of fourteen then, remember!"

"Of course." Almeria felt abashed as she always did when she had said something foolish: She was sure this remark had revealed how old she considered him. He was in fact only four years her senior. This trivial set back thrust her into one of her tongue-tied silences which, luckily, Frances broke. Almeria had sought her help over any awkwardness in talking with Mr Tiffen, before they had set out for the theatre. Fanny had agreed, "But you must not leave all responsibility for conversation with me. I know you of old!" Merry had given her word, of course, but the reality was as difficult as ever: her mind was a blank. What could she find to say to this rather staid gentleman when Frances ceased talking?

She glanced out of the corner of her eye at the still-empty box on her right, noticing at the same time that there were not many people in the theatre at all, considering how late it was. Now *that* was something to remark upon, at least, she thought. She turned to Mr Tiffen, who said immediately:

"Your cousin was just observing how thin the audience is tonight, particularly as the one-act play should have started these five minutes past."

Almeria agreed, and fell into a crushed and almost resentful silence. But still, if the evening progressed in this deadly manner, she reflected, she would be glad it was her last taste of society for months to come. She roused herself to pay heed to what her neighbour was saying to her.

". . . take the opportunity to say how charming you are looking tonight, Almeria."

"Thank you," she murmured, the blush spreading from her already rosy cheeks: it was no use, she could not act the brazen hussy—or even the mildest of flirts—with the earnest Mr Tiffen.

She gave an almost audible sigh of relief when the curtain rose at last upon the first play. However, her contentment was short-lived: an actor with quite the most strident voice she had ever heard took command of the stage; the audience became steadily more restless and noisy; and, to complete her discomfort, the heat from the eight-candle chandelier suspended from the front of their box was quite overpowering. She wished fervently she had begun her decline that morning. . . .

She was sunk in gloomy contemplation of the tedious hours stretching before her—as she had by now quite lost interest in *Romeo and Juliet*—when a movement to the right took her attention. Yes . . . it was Old Harry! Her heart thumped with the excitement—and the heat—and she hoped she may not faint. She fanned herself agitatedly and forced her attention back to the stage and its solitary bellowing occupant.

Really, she thought presently, this must be a one-actor play as well as a one-act one, then wondered why she could never think of remarks like that when they were needed. The audience continued fidgety, and she noticed Harry and his friend seemed to be searching the boxes for someone, so she dare not watch them overtly. But the next time she looked back, when the short play had just finished, he had gone and the friend was on his own. He had presumably found the person he was seeking and had hastened to join them.

"The audience seems uncommonly boisterous tonight," commented Mr Tiffen, looking up at the gesticulating crowd hanging over the brass rail of the gallery.

Almeria thought she detected a note of apprehension, and with the confidence of a seasoned play-goer sought to reassure him. "It is the oppressive atmosphere, I fancy, it must be monstrously hot up there. The belated start and that quite dreadful play has done nothing to improve their mood, but we are perfectly secure here."

"To be sure we are," he agreed, looking even more apprehensively into the pit below, where an abundance of space and the absence of a forty-foot drop gave rise to more ambitious rioting than in the gallery. The orange peel began to fly and was soon joined by assorted hats, sticks and other missiles.

Mrs Denbury was heard to comment it was exactly what she had always expected to see at the theatre and could not imagine why anyone should want to make a habit of visiting such places. "We must certainly quit before the half-price mob is admitted later," she declared.

No one was inclined to argue against this proposal, although Almeria had hoped that for once they might stay to the end of the performance so that she might see where Harry went. Another quick look at his box confirmed that he had now returned —but he was standing up and appeared to be having a slight altercation with his companion. Her attention was quickly diverted from all thought of Harry and his doings by a sudden fusillade of missiles cascading upon them.

All was confusion: Theodosia screamed and Mrs Denbury clasped her to her bosom; Mr Tiffen leapt up and then sat down again; Mr Denbury leapt up and stayed up, leaning over the balcony and muttering, "What the devil's here?"

In reply a rotten apple soared past his ear and landed in his wife's puce satin lap, followed by other assorted fruity offerings.

"Mr Denbury," she shrieked, "do something for pity's sake—we have strayed into Bedlam!"

"No need, my dear—I think some fellow has them under control now."

Only Frances and Almeria had remained calm during this onslaught, and Frances said: "It was merely fruit, was it not? Is any damage done?"

"It certainly is!" cried Mrs Denbury. "Look at my dress—it is quite ruined!"

In the meantime *Romeo and Juliet* had claimed

the attention of at least part of the audience, but
Almeria was not of their number: she was staring
at the gentleman who had quelled the rioters—it
was Harry, and she noticed for the first time he had
a slight limp. For a moment she wondered if she
had been cherishing a passion for Lord Byron
himself but commonsense soon dispelled this fanciful notion: he had none of the plump looks of that
notorious gentleman. He turned and looked up at
the Denburys' box, seemed to smile directly at Almeria then vanished from her sight.

"I'd like to thank the fellow," said Mr Denbury,
making his way back to his seat. "Wonder who he
is?"

"Never mind who he is. It would be folly to set
foot outside the box," declared his wife, dabbing at
the stained satin.

There was still a background of noise and discontent from the audience despite the appearance of
Romeo himself, and Mrs Denbury's voice continued
to be heard above all.

"If I did not have a lively fear I should be set
upon I would go down to the Saloon for a restora-
tive. I cannot hear one word of the play, nor can I
see more than a glimpse of the players' heads from
time to time."

This querulous speech drew offers from all sides:
Mr Denbury to sally forth to the Saloon for re-
freshments, and Mr Tiffen, half-standing once more,
to offer his place to his hostess.

Almeria was oblivious to all this bustle as Old Harry had not returned to his box, but instead the friend had this moment gone, too.

Mrs Denbury declined all offers of help, and her husband said a little testily that if they did not cease their fussing more missiles would come their way, but from neighbouring boxes this time.

A knock on the door silenced them all. A young lad came in with a note and handed it to Mr Denbury.

"Wait, boy . . . Here, I can't read it in this light. Merry, you've the brightest spot there."

She took the paper and had no difficulty with the pencilled bold hand. She read it out in a low voice. 'Permit me to offer my regrets for the unpleasant incident in the pit. I trust no damage was inflicted other than the obvious distress of the ladies of your party. I should deem it an honour if you would take some refreshment with me in the Saloon during the next interval. Your obedient servant, Henry Chirton.'

"Must be the fellow I saw—very good in him. Yes, boy, convey my thanks to the gentleman—we'll be glad to accept his invitation."

Almeria had scarcely had time to invest this happy accident with the romantic significance it clearly deserved, when her mother's voice intruded.

"*You* may accept his invitation, Mr Denbury, but I fear *we* shall not. Theo and I have had more than enough of this evening's entertainment. Perhaps you would be good enough to summon the carriage. I'm sure Mr Tiffen will be glad to escort us home."

The gentleman thus appealed to turned hastily in his chair. "Oh, of course, yes m-m-ma'am. You're very wise. It is for all the world like being in the stocks waited to be pelted, is it not? The ladies should not be exposed to such indignity."

"I don't mind in the least," Almeria protested. "Besides, nothing of this nature has ever occurred before, has it, papa? And we are so high up here it is most unlikely it will happen again."

But no one paid any attention to her: they never did.

The carriage was sent for and in vain Almeria tried to think of a way to stay behind but she could think of nothing. Quite dumb-founded by the cruel vagaries of fate, she followed her mother and sister down the stairs. Mr Tiffen was so struck by her dashed expression he was sufficiently emboldened to take her arm in support. "Pray don't take it too much to heart, Almeria, we shall have many more evenings together, I promise you."

Unhearing, she smiled at him and didn't even trouble to withdraw her arm. Frances noticed this significant gesture and was pleased something good had come out of the disastrous evening.

When Mr Denbury's carriage had disappeared round the corner into Drury Lane—but not before

—Major Crispin Maunby permitted himself to laugh, and when he did, it halted his and Harry's progress down Russell-street for quite a minute. "Y-your f-face when that worthy gentleman arrived at the assignation alone—I'll never forget it!"

"It has its humour, certainly," admitted Harry, "but there is no cause to fall into convulsions. A tentative connexion has been forged—we have exchanged cards, and it is my intention to call upon the ladies of the Denbury establishment in the morning to see how they go on after their upsetting experience. All within the bounds of what is seemly— as you put it—is it not?"

"Perfectly so," gasped a pink-faced Crispin, recovering his breath a little, "but is inciting a riot in the pit quite so proper, I wonder?" he asked innocently, beginning to walk in an aimless fashion towards Henrietta-street.

Harry limped after him. "My dear fellow, I *quelled* a riot—single-handed, no less—you saw me do it."

"Ay, so I did," grinned Crispin, "but you'll not gammon me, Harry! Your tame rascals in the pit had the devil's own work to pitch their ammunition so high as the second tier."

Harry's insouciance faltered at last and he frowned. "Did it look so particular, then?"

"Only to me, I daresay, but then I know your wicked ways, Old Harry, don't I?"

"Denbury seemed genuinely grateful I must say—"

"Don't fret, I'd go bail he nurses no suspicions of your dark designs upon the females in his family."

"We are looking for a female for *you*, if you remember."

More swiftly on cue than the players had been at the theatre, a woman darted out from a doorway and laid a detaining hand on Crispin's arm, bestowing upon him a yellowing smile and a haze of gin fumes.

He dismissed her goodnaturedly, and answered Harry. "Maybe so, but it will give an odd appearance if we should *both* call on the Denburys tomorrow, surely? You were the gallant rescuer after all."

Harry weighed the sense of this as, somewhat belatedly, they passed a stern-looking gentleman seated in their path holding aloft a board which declared in bold letters 'Beware of Bad Houses'.

"Yes, you may be right—perhaps we must dismiss this initial foray as yielding little but experience—nonetheless, I have undertaken to call at Bedford Square tomorrow, and call I will. They were, as I suspected, people of good standing."

"Yes," agreed Crispin almost wistfully, "I own that a Nabob's daughter would not have come amiss at this time."

"Well, we cannot be certain that the lady who took your eye *was* his daughter—there was a cousin present, I collect, as well as his two girls."

They had reached the junction with Bedford-street now, and came to a halt.

"Where are we going?" demanded Crispin. "Have you the least notion?"

"Why no, I was following you . . . We might look in at Watier's first," he announced with a bland air.

"Capital idea!" Crispin brightened considerably.

". . . to record our wager in their betting book, I thought."

The look of cheerful anticipation faded. "You're hoaxing me—you wouldn't be so Gothic!"

Harry grinned and slapped his friend on the shoulder. "Of course I wouldn't, you old griffin— besides I have your word as a gentleman on that, don't I? That's enough for me. Come along, we're wasting time."

5

"I shall urge your papa in the strongest fashion to discontinue these theatre visits of yours, Almeria," Mrs Denbury had said, almost as soon as they had closed the carriage door on Covent Garden Theatre. "They are as unwholesome as they are unnecessary, don't you agree, Mr Tiffen?" She was at the time pulling down the blinds of the carriage windows to shut out the scenes of degradation endemic to the area, and which otherwise might have sullied her daughters' innocent gaze. It was a precaution her husband had never thought of taking with Almeria so was a trifle wasted.

Mr Tiffen, thus appealed to by his future mother-in-law, could do nothing but concur although he did express the opinion that they had been a little unfortunate perhaps.

In the ordinary way, Almeria would have joined battle and fought for her theatre visits, but as she had decided this was to be her last appearance in the world for some time she made no protest.

Frances looked at her anticipating a violent reaction, and when none was forthcoming she taxed her with her silence when they returned home and Mr Tiffen had gone. "I am sorry this evening's events have deprived you of your plays, Merry; I know you do love them so. I quite thought you would raise your voice in protest at the harshness of the ban."

Almeria, whose sole gain from the evening so far was the discovery of Harry's real name, said listlessly, "I think mama is right. Tonight's events have merely given me the headache. I will go up to bed, I think, if you will excuse me, Fanny."

She was longing to know what her father would think of Harry, of course, but it might be hours before he came home, and it would not do to show an excessive interest in the stranger. Next morning, the onset of her decline was postponed yet again for, by now, she had decided that *something* might come out of that chance encounter. It would mean she would have to attend their card-party that evening, but she could tell herself it might be the last time she had to face Mr Tiffen. However, she must not forget that his proposal of marriage could be imminent, and the embarrassment of that interview had to be avoided at all costs.

Almeria was not late to the breakfast table but nonetheless her father had left already for some important meeting at East India House. But Theo and Mrs Denbury were there, still, and no sooner had Almeria joined them when a note was brought in by the butler for her mother.

"Now, isn't that too provoking of him—Gerald Winterton has cried off for tonight. So we are a gentleman short," she announced, casting the unwelcome note amongst the silver.

"Two gentlemen short," supplemented Theo, over her cup of chocolate. "You forget that Mr Plumptree will not be coming either."

Mrs Denbury stared at her daughter. "I am not sure I was ever aware of it."

"Why yes, it was contained in an oblique fashion in his note left at the theatre last night. In effect he cancelled all his immediate engagements but hoped to escort me to the Mertons' ball next week, if you please!" Theo's dark eyes flashed indignantly.

"I do hope that young man is not wavering in his attentions. When we tried to fix the date of the wedding he was as slippery as an eel in oil. Oh, I know he had some apparently credible tale of the house at Richmond not being ready. You have not even seen it yet, have you, Theo?"

"No, not one brick of it." Mr Plumptree had promised most faithfully that she should see it the moment the alterations had been completed and not before—but Theo was already bored with her betrothed: it had been a challenge to bring him to the point but since then she had steadily lost interest.

"Well, we must not be over hasty. He is the eldest son of a family of the first respectability and substance, although I did hear a hint of a cotton manufactory connexion in the Midlands."

"That is where the substance comes from, I expect," interposed Almeria, becoming increasingly impatient with her family's pretensions; after all, what was her father but a merchant? But she regretted her remark—as she usually did: it merely drew attention to herself.

"We can manage very well without your ill-considered observations on the matter, Almeria. Mr Tiffen, I am pleased to say, shows no such regrettable tendency to vacillate, and I have every intention of granting his wish for a private word with you. He, at least, has not cried off for this evening."

At this point Frances joined them, with profuse apologies for being late. "It was essential I should mend a great rent in my only clean morning gown if I was to appear with any semblance of decency."

"But Travers would have done that for you, Fanny," Mrs Denbury said at once: she had always shown the greatest kindness to her bereaved niece.

"I know she would, aunt, but there is no call to trouble your people. It is wholly my fault—I have allowed my wardrobe to run down sadly. I have lacked the interest, you know, in recent years to refurbish it." A sad little smile hovered about her lips, then she went on with determination, "but I am quite resolved to remedy the matter this very day."

Almeria thought what a sweet face her cousin had and, not for the first time, she raged inwardly against the cruel stroke of fate which had widowed her so young. "If you are travelling into the town this morning, Fanny, may I accompany you? I must change my library books." She wanted to deposit a long list at the circulating library so that she would be well-supplied whilst she languished at home in future weeks.

"Books!" her mother cried in exasperation. "What do you need with books, now?"

"I thought I would borrow a volume on domestic economy and the management of servants," Almeria said meekly.

"Oh, I see," responded Mrs Denbury, momentarily at a loss; then she reverted to the subject of her depleted whist-party.

* * *

Mrs Denbury had not seen the gentleman at Covent Garden whom her husband had been so anxious to meet, and consequently had taken little interest in her spouse's subsequent favourable reports of his encounter. She knew he had a tendency to see good in all men and therefore dismissed their unknown deliverer as an encroaching but well-intentioned bore.

Consequently her over-riding emotion was one of irritation when Morgan, their dour Welsh butler, interrupted her deliberations with Theo regarding suitable unattached gentlemen for the whist-party. She regarded the name on the card proffered by the servant. "Sir Henry Chirton, Baronet," she muttered.

"Mr Denbury intimated the gentleman might possibly call this morning, ma'am. His visit is consequent upon their meeting at Covent Garden last night, I understand."

"Yes, I remember the name now. Either he possesses a quite extraordinary degree of punctilio or is a sycophantic proser who lacks an audience." She consulted Morgan. "Which do you judge him to be?"

"All I can say, ma'am, is that he has the air of a young gentleman of the first consequence, but there is nothing of a dandified nature to him."

"Young?" She exchanged an involuntary glance with Theo. "Well, you may show him in, Morgan."

She hastened over to the mirror to ensure her cap was straight. "A baronetcy may signify nothing, of course, and one can never tell with your papa—he collects acquaintances like a dog hoards bones."

"And Morgan considers anyone under fifty to be a babe-in-arms," giggled Theo, but she was disposing herself carefully by the window all the same, and checking that none of her long dark ringlets had strayed out of place.

When the door opened to admit their visitor she was exceedingly glad she had made the effort, for a more sublime-looking gentleman she had rarely seen. By the time her roguish eyes met his when he was introduced, they had noted and approved his faultless apparel (not the least dandified as Morgan had said), his impressive height, and his air of easy assurance. The voice, too, excited interest; it was, she hazarded, the well-modulated one of a singer, and already thoughts of duets flitted through her mind—she had a pretty voice herself, everyone said so, and Plumptree couldn't sing. She decided Sir Henry's limp was but the slightest affliction and merely added to his attractions. The frank and apparently approving manner in which he viewed her won her admiration at once: here was a gentleman worthy of her fast languishing skills in flirtation.

For Theo this pert perusal was in no way singular, but for Harry, on the other hand, the agreeable assessment was a novelty: he thought he was going to enjoy his self-assumed role of match-maker. Reluctantly he relinquished the dark, long-lashed gaze and turned his attention to the parent. Such was his address that in no time at all he had quite won her over. The events of the previous night were the prime topic of conversation, of course, and in response to his quite touching concern she made light of her spoiled opera gown, even going so far as to confide in him the methods Travers had used in an endeavour to restore it to its original state. "But it is nothing, nothing at all. I do not regard it."

"It would please me greatly to be able to compensate wholly for your misfortune by replacing
the dress—" he could see his hostess wavering on
the verge of outrage "—but then, that would never
serve, would it?" He favoured her with his most
devastating smile. "However, if you would permit
me I can suggest a most efficacious remedy for
spoiled silk—potato water: it never fails."

Mrs Denbury was a trifle bewildered by this gentleman of undoubted charm who veered from the
almost indecorous to the positively domestic in one
breath, and she did not pause to reflect how he
might know so much about silks—a material little
worn by gentlemen. However, she thanked him
profusely and charged Theo to remember the receipt.

The next few minutes were dedicated to the deplorable habits of the play-going masses, and ended
with Mrs Denbury asserting that she for one had
not the slightest wish to set foot in a theatre again.

Harry felt his guilt beginning to accumulate: first
a nigh-on ruined gown and now a lifetime habit of
play-going brought to an untimely end. He could
not be aware that his hostess had never held the
theatre in high regard. Quite at a stand to know how
to redress these ills he said: "I am sorry to hear
that, ma'am, but I feel sure you need not fear a
recurrence of last night's incident," he finished with
justifiable conviction.

"Oh, no matter, Sir Henry, I'd as lief stay home and play whist and that's the truth."

"Ah, do I understand that we share an addiction to the tables, ma'am?"

Theo, who had been watching their visitor enrapt and in silence hitherto, suddenly said: "Mama, could we not ask Sir Henry to join us this evening for our card-party?"

"I'm sure he would find it tedious beyond words, my love, and in any event I daresay he is promised elsewhere."

But there was just enough of the interrogative in the latter remark to enable Harry to grasp at the opportunity offered. "Oh, no, I should count it a great honour, I do assure you, but I have not the least wish to intrude upon a private gathering."

"The case is this, sir, I have been sadly let down only this morning by two of my prospective guests and I should indeed be grateful if you could see your way to easing my problem. A whist-party which lacks partners is but a sorry affair!"

"Why, I should be delighted!" As indeed he would, he thought: he could salve his conscience and forward his scheme at one and the same time, it seemed. Even his Argyle Rooms engagement must take second place to this. "I have no wife to complete your numbers, I fear," he added, apparently light-heartedly but the ploy paid dividends.

"Oh, but we are still a *gentleman* short," exclaimed Theo, immensely relieved to hear of the non-existence of a Lady Chirton.

"Well, we can scarcely expect Sir Henry to solve all our problems, Theo."

The opportunity was too good to miss, of course, and at the risk of being thought pushing he secured an invitation for Crispin without further ado. Thus his call was completed with the utmost satisfaction to all parties and he took his leave of the ladies shortly afterwards.

Almeria, on her return home from the shopping expedition with Fanny, when she was apprised of this news by a voluble and thrasonic Theo (for she was perfectly certain that she alone had captivated Sir Henry with her irresistible charm) went first the colour of beetroot and then quite pale.

"Sir Henry Chirton?—he's coming *here,* tonight?" she gasped out finally.

"Well, that *is* what I've just been saying: but I can't see why you should find it so startling. After all, you've never met him, have you? Oh, you needn't worry, he'll not take any notice of you. In any event, you can cling to Mr Tiffen's coat-tails now, if either of the gentlemen shows the least inclination to flirt with you—which I'm perfectly sure they won't!"

The rest of the afternoon was an ordeal for Almeria: she suffered such a crisis of nerves that she began to wish she had never heard of Old Harry. But she resolved to see it through, and to behave as far as possible in a perfectly unexceptionable manner: that way she might pass wholly unnoticed. To further that end she decided to wear the decorous

primrose and white dress. However, when she came
to look for her pearl necklace to wear with it she
could not find it anywhere, so she chose the amber
instead. Theo would doubtless attract Harry's attention: she was clearly very taken with him and
most likely would flirt outrageously with him as
Mr Plumptree was absent.

Which was exactly what happened. But, as Almeria noticed to her astonishment, Theo was not the
only female to set her cap that evening, for there
was Fanny laughing with Major Crispin Maunby
as she had not laughed since coming to Bedford
Square years ago. Almeria was pleased that by a
happy chance Fanny had only that morning in-
dulged herself in the most fetching gown of sap-
phire blue, which with her shining blonde hair made
her look like a young girl.

"Your cousin is in glowing good looks tonight,"
commented Mr Tiffen, with more enthusiasm than
was customary, and who had noticed his companion's eye upon Frances. "They make an attractive
couple, indeed. But who is the gentleman with her?
I did not catch his name, I'm afraid."

"He is a Major Maunby, I believe," Almeria told
him, "a friend of the gentleman whom papa met at
Covent Garden last night." She found it easier not
to say his name for some reason.

"Oh yes, the dashing Lothario over there. I dare
swear he leaves a trail of broken hearts wherever he
goes. Your sister, Theo's, will be amongst them if

she does not take care." There was a note of disapproval in his voice.

"She is only acting out of pique, I dare say, because she feels Mr Plumptree is neglecting her of late." Almeria did not know why she should defend Theo, for she had suffered a quite unnecessary humiliation at her hands when Sir Henry was first introduced to her. As if it were not trial enough to be face to face with Harry at last, Theo had to be the one to introduce them; she had shadowed the visitor since his arrival. "This is my sister, Almeria —the shy young Denbury," she had added gratuitously, as Almeria knew she was scarlet with embarrassment already. "No one could dub you so, ma'am," Harry had retorted in quiet but austere accents which would have crushed Almeria, but Theo had taken it as the highest compliment.

After this ill-starred beginning Almeria had exchanged several commonplaces with Harry, or at least answered monosyllabically to his enquiries, obviously designed to set her at ease but doomed to failure. He was shepherded away by Theo almost the instant Mr Tiffen had joined them.

When the tables were set up for whist Almeria elected to be a spectator on this occasion, even if it did mean conversing with Mr Tiffen: that must be preferable to taking the risk of playing whist with Harry and making a dreadful bungle of the game. Her abstention meant a gentleman was not needed to partner her and to her surprise Major Maunby decided to sit out: it soon became clear why. He and Frances, seated well away from the card-playing company, were quickly sunk in the most earnest of dialogues. Almeria positioned herself away from them but where she had the clearest view of Harry. She was not near any candelabra, and was able to study him to her heart's content at much closer quarters than usual. He had, she soon discovered, an endearing habit of creasing up his molasses-dark eyes when he laughed—and he did laugh a great deal. In her moonstruck state she thought his longish curling hair looked for all the world like the black silky coat of Cordelia's spaniel. She tried not to make invidious comparisons with poor Mr Tiffen who, although of similar colouring had much less prepossessing features, recalling her father's remark that one didn't choose one's face, but it was no use: to her Harry was a beau-ideal and she was vastly relieved that closer scrutiny had not dashed this conception. But it was more than outward appearance which influenced her, as she was well aware; there had not been the least sense of rapprochement when she had met Mr. Tiffen, but although even now she had scarcely exchanged above a dozen words with Harry she had a remarkable sense of affinity with him. As she possessed a great deal of gumption—inherited from her northern father—the strength of this feeling for Harry did not blind her to the absurdity of a shy greenhead girl entertaining such sentiments about a desirable but determined bachelor, who had without

question, as Mr Tiffen had remarked, left a trail
of shattered hopes—and mamas—behind him . . .

He was not partnered by Theo: Mrs Denbury had
decided that her daughter's behaviour was in danger
of going beyond the bounds of what was permissible
—certainly in one betrothed to another, however
precariously. So she sequestered Sir Henry to herself, and together they challenged her husband and
a boisterous matronly lady possessed of formidable
card-playing skills. Thus, it was perfectly natural
for Almeria to watch this contest with the greatest
interest, and Mr Tiffen had to be satisfied
with the most desultory conversation snatched between games. It was a close run thing, the first two
games of the rubber being shared, and it was not
until the last game, which went to Harry and her
mama, that Almeria felt it incumbent upon her to
pay attention to the spectators in preference to the
players. Mr Tiffen seemed anxious that Frances
should not make herself look too particular by being
tête-à-tête with the unknown major, and he and
Almeria strolled across to them.

Frances immediately broke off what she was saying and raised an animated face to the new-come
pair. "You must think me lost to all sense of conduct but Major Maunby and I have been having
the most interesting conversation." She favoured
her companion with a quick shy smile, and added,
"Well, I have found it so—I must not speak for
him."

Crispin hastened to assure her that he had indeed

found it an uncommonly agreeable encounter, whilst Mr Tiffen looked on a trifle bleakly, Almeria thought: he was, she was beginning to realise, a high-stickler for punctilio.

It was he who broke the brief silence which descended upon the group. "You were at Covent Garden last night, I collect, m-m-major. Were you involved in that unfortunate fracas in the pit?" he asked conversationally.

This innocent remark had the effect of disconcerting Crispin. "Er—no, not exactly. Sir Henry was responsible for that—for putting an end to it, that is."

"I think the whole affair has been refined upon too much," Almeria was moved to say. "In all my years of play-going it is the first time anything of the kind has happened. Oh, there has been fighting in the pit, of course, but they have never before used the occupants of the boxes as Aunt Sallys. I do not suppose it would happen again."

"Really, Merry, to hear you speak one would suppose you were a positive greybeard. 'All your years of playgoing' indeed!" Fanny said teasingly.

"Well, I have been visiting the theatre for four and a half years," she retorted meticulously, always uncertain of herself in company and therefore quite bereft of her usual sense of humour.

"You must have witnessed the volcanic Mr Kean's rapid rise to fame, I collect?" Crispin said.

"Oh yes, I think I have seen all his most famous portrayals—including Richard the Third."

"It was the greatest pity he did not play Romeo last night," Frances remarked, "the audience would have been more attentive and less inclined to run amuck, I dare say."

"Ah, but then he won't, you see," Crispin explained. "I have heard Mr Kean declare he will have none of the milk-and-water roles—not at any price."

"You are acquainted with Mr Kean, are you, sir?" asked Almeria, forgetting her shyness momentarily.

"But slightly—after all I have been in town only for a month or more, but I have seen him occasionally in the Harp Tavern, you know, hard by Drury Lane. Anyway, Sir Henry is your man if you are interested in any aspect of the sock and buskin, ma'am. You would appear to have much in common."

This speech drew a blush from Almeria and a frown from Mr Tiffen. Luckily at that point the whole group's attention was claimed by a minor uproar at one of the whist tables. Mrs Denbury and Sir Henry had won yet another rubber, and there were cries of outrage from Mr Denbury and his voluble but highly-skilled partner.

"I can see, Sir Henry, that it was a stroke of the greatest good fortune which led you to our rescue last night," his hostess said, flushed with triumph and delight. "I cannot remember when last I routed Mr Denbury so completely!"

~~~~~~ 6 ~~~~~~

Harry had not contrived the meeting with the Denburys solely that Mrs Denbury might have the
satisfaction of vanquishing her spouse at the whist
table, and as he walked homewards with Crispin
afterwards he wondered if his new-found aim of
match-making was flourishing.

They were strolling under the stars in the direction
of Soho Square where Harry lived, and Crispin had
lodgings not far away from him in Thrift-street.
Apart from the passing of an occasional hackney
carriage or family coach Great Russell-street was
quiet, and so were the two gentlemen for a minute
or two.

Crispin was the first to speak. "Well, I never thought to see Old Harry, the scourge of Watier's, playing whist at a guinea a rubber and—what's more—seeming to enjoy it. Did you?" He sounded incredulous.

"To tell the truth, I did. It was the sort of small convivial gathering I have not attended of late. Made me realise what a dead bore the routs and squeezes are during the season."

"Ah well, that's the terrible penalty you pay for being such an irresistible *parti*," Crispin said in mock commiseration. "These mamas never give up, do they?"

Harry's laugh echoed round the darkened houses. "By George, they don't, but I have their measure now—I've survived another season unscathed. But come, I want to know what *you* thought to the company tonight. You didn't join us at cards but I'll not believe you eschewed the temptation of the tables, at a mere guinea a rubber, just because you let slip a monkey at Watier's last night."

Crispin's smooth features puckered in distaste.

"The company was not as bad as that, surely?" Harry said.

"No, of course it wasn't, lunkhead, but I had rather you didn't remind me of last night, if you please." But then he gave a shout of laughter. "You're a deep-dyed rogue, Harry! I swear you led me to Watier's last night like a lamb to the slaughter. Yes, you may stare, but admit that if I'm adrift in

Dun Territory I'm in a fair way to being riveted to the first female I set eyes on. *Then* you may have the satisfaction of winning your wager!"

Harry had listened to this imputation with a deepening frown. "Hold hard, Cris, I mislike the sound of that! First, *you* were the one to propose Watier's if I recollect aright, and second, I am not so sunk in iniquity that I would have *you* outrun the constable for *my* paltry wager."

"Hey, let's not come to points over this! I was only hoaxing you. As if I would saddle you with responsibility for my debts. You must think me a shabster . . . No," he went on more calmly, "in the event, I am glad I came with you to Bedford Square tonight—it was a pleasant diversion from my problems. But, mark you, I'd rather not know how you contrived the invitation."

"But I told you—"

"So you did, but you hardly expect me to believe that flim-flam—*two* gentlemen short indeed! Ha! No, you took a fancy to young Miss Theodosia, and in your inimitable and devious way secured the invitations. I'm perfectly sure I was only included as a sort of chaperon," he concluded with a gleam in his eye.

"I did not take a fancy—as you put it so inelegantly—to anyone!" exploded Harry, and was prepared to enlarge upon his objections to Crispin's speech, but was interrupted.

"Well, that young lady was certainly casting sheep's eyes at you, you can't deny it."

"Why should I? That is quite another matter. I am not to be held responsible for the actions of every shatter-brained coming baggage who casts lures in my direction." There was a brief and appalled silence, then he said anxiously, "You were not yourself interested—I mean you did not consider she—"

"For the lord's sake, Harry, let me put you out of your misery!" he chuckled. "No, I share your views upon the lady in question."

"So that sets the seal on my expectations of the Denbury family," Harry sighed. "The other ladies, I understand, are already committed."

"Oh no, you are out there, surely?"

"Am I? Well, not so far as the fair-complexioned young lady is concerned. Almeria, I think her name is—or the shy young Denbury as her sister, Theodosia, kindly informed me. What florid names they are all blessed with, incidentally! Still, it is small wonder the child is shy with a sister like that putting her to the blush all the while. Nonetheless, as that same sister told me somewhat sharply, the girl is betrothed to the Friday-faced fellow, a budding clergyman, I collect. A more ill-assorted pair you couldn't wish to see, for there was a sense of fun about *her* eyes and a humorous quirk to the mouth which all her want of confidence could not suppress."

"Hallo!" said Crispin, "Do I detect a note of sentiment creeping into the old libertine's voice?"

"Cheese it, Jack-sauce!" Harry advised, but without rancour. "No, it merely pains me to see such a melancholy instance of an unpropitious match."

"I wouldn't care to speculate upon that, but you may be right about the girl. She showed a markedly unclerical and lively interest in the stage, and I referred her to you as being the fount of knowledge on such matters."

"Did you indeed? I'll wager Friday-face did not care for that! But we have wandered from the point," he went on briskly. "You were suggesting that there was a Denbury daughter unattached, were you not?"

"There's an unattached lady to be sure but not, I think, a Denbury, although she looks very much like a sister to the fair girl. She is Mrs Wren, a cousin of the family."

"Is there no Mr Wren?"

"No, he was a captain in the 3rd Division, killed at Cuidad Rodrigo, his wife told me, in that damnable explosion which carried off General Mackinnon."

"Good God, yes, I remember that day well enough," Harry said sober-faced. "I was unhorsed by the concussion from that same explosion. How devilish cold it was, too!" He thought for a moment. "No, I don't recall the name, do you?"

"Yes, I did know him—oh, not very well, but enough to know his worth and be able to give some solace to his widow by talking about him."

This turn in the conversation inevitably led them

to discuss their shared experiences in the Peninsula campaign, but all the while Harry was assailed by a feeling of unease about the events he had set into motion the previous night: suppose Crispin did marry this Mrs Wren?—and on the face of it there was no reason why he should not. They were of an age, he would hazard, and Cris had displayed both interest and concern in her. Marriages had sprung from less than that, he reflected . . . but if it foundered, how would he feel then? And, as she was not a Denbury daughter she presumably would not bring him a share of the Nabob's fortune. Harry soon convinced himself that his friend would be as well-advised to marry the tyrannical but wealthy Meg Venables as a chance-met lady; but he could scarcely back out of his wager now, not with a thousand pounds at stake for Crispin, who obviously needed to win it more desperately than ever after last night's losses. He must endeavour *not* to find any more prospective wives—it was too risky —and he must discourage his friend's pursuit of Mrs Wren, if he was pursuing her . . .

"Was Mrs Wren the lady who took your eye in the box party last night?" Harry interposed baldly and without warning, not hearing a word as Crispin relived a particularly agonising episode for him in the Peninsula war, when he had a violent eruption of boils.

"—never had a ride like that in all my days: the road to Bajados, it was—What was that?" He turned a glazed expression to his friend. "Oh, Mrs Wren . . . Harry! you're fishing!" he said in warning tones. "Yes, she was, but I shall tell you no more—it was not part of the wager, as I recall, that I should give you a round-by-round account of the success—or failure—of your efforts to make an April-gentleman of me."

"Yes, you are quite right, of course," admitted a somewhat chastened Harry, who was beginning to regret his rash interference in Crispin's affairs.

"On New Year's Eve, and not before, you shall know the outcome—unless I am so bowled over by one of the ladies of your choice that I can't wait till then to be leg-shackled," he said sardonically.

"Do I take it then, that you will attend the ball next week for which Mrs Denbury is so anxious to procure invitations on our behalf?" Harry asked, ignoring the sarcasm.

"Why not? It is devilish dull now the season has finished, and there are few enough entertainments of any description in evidence anywhere. Besides, just think of all the unattached females I might encounter there, with every other gentleman left town for the shooting by that time! Who knows what might come of it?" Crispin said in jaunty accents.

Harry certainly didn't know, and hoped devoutly nothing would.

The bell of the watchman rang as they reached Soho Square. "One of the clock and a fair night, and all's w-e-ll!" came the familiar cry.

"Lord, it's as late as that, is it?" Crispin exclaimed. "I hope Flutter isn't hunched over his candle waiting to give me one of his jobations on late hours and loose living," he said morosely.

"He never does! Why, he's only a retired butler, isn't he, even if he is the proprietor of the house. Anyway, you must have given him a harassing time these past weeks!"

"Yes, it's wearing us both to the bone!"

"Crispin, why don't you move in with me? You know you're welcome. Indeed, I would have asked you when you first came back to England but I had no notion you would be fixed in town for so long." Apart from a genuine wish for his company, Harry saw this as a welcome way to help his friend over his financial difficulties.

Crispin demurred. "It's good of you, Harry, but I don't care to impose upon you."

"Fustian rubbish! How can you impose when I am alone in this great house? And you may come and go as you please. I give my word Tobin shan't lecture you whatever scrapes you fall into. He is the very soul of discretion or he would not have survived in my household for so long!"

"I can believe that! Yes, thank you, I'd like to accept. You're a great gun, Harry."

They had arrived at Harry's door. "Will you come in?"

"I think not. I can't wait to confront Flutter now!"

"Goodnight to you, then . . . Oh, Cris," Harry

added in a hesitant, low voice, "you're not so badly dipped that you're contemplating approaching the Ten Tribes, are you? Because if you are," he went on urgently, "you would apply to me first, wouldn't you?"

"No, matters ain't as black as that—but you'd best act governor with me for the next few weeks and keep me from the tables. My pockets would be to let after another night like the last one! Even so, I'd not ask *you* to raise the wind. No, I'd have no alternative then but to find me a Golden Dolly— but *not* Meg Venables, so you would stand to win your wager!" he concluded with great spirit, and left a thoughtful Harry mounting the steps to his door.

Frances was searching the pages of back-numbers of the *Lady's Magazine* for a particular embroidery design for a border.

"I'd swear it appeared about two years ago," she said to Almeria, as she turned the pages of the bound volume. "Well, I didn't know that, did you, Merry? 'The coffin of Charles I was opened in the presence of the Regent,'" she read, " 'the body was wrapped in a waxed cloth, and not at all decayed: the features, the cut of the beard &c. exactly agreeing with the portraits which are known to be true likenesses'. Henry VIII's tomb was also opened— oh, but that only contained the skull and limb bones." This, she knew, was just the kind of item which normally took her young cousin's attention, and she was surprised when there was no response. "I wonder what the Regent's feelings were? It must have been an eeriesome experience."

"Mm, I read it at the time, I fancy," Almeria said at last, but didn't raise her head from her stitchery.

"There's precious little you *haven't* read, is there?" Frances responded.

"Except Domestic Economy and the Management of Servants," Almeria couldn't resist saying.

"Oh yes, that was rather wicked of you, Merry! Your poor mama was quite speechless . . . And what in fact did you carry from the library—a volume of Lord Byron, was it not?" she asked with a smile.

"Yes, *The Corsair*." Almeria was not overfond of poetry but the fleeting confusion of Harry with Byron had lingered in her mind, and besides she thought Mr Tiffen would surely recoil from the impropriety of a Byron-reading wife.

"Ah, that's the one," cried Frances with satisfaction. She took the volume to the table in order to trace the design. "What did you think of the two surprise guests last night?" she asked presently.

"They were well enough, I suppose," mumbled Almeria into her embroidery.

"You scarcely noticed them, I expect, but I found Major Maunby so easy to converse with, and with quite a rare understanding."

"How do you associate with strangers on such terms of cordiality after only a brief acquaintance,

I should like to know?" Almeria asked quite bitterly: she felt sure if she had had Frances' ability it would have enabled her to establish a relationship with Harry—however tenuous; as it was she might never have been in the same room with him for hours on end.

"In general terms I can't really say." She paused in her tracing. "But the major knew my late husband, it seems, and that was an immediate bond, as you may imagine."

"Yes, I see," said Almeria, pleased for Fanny, but not finding it much help to her own situation. The question was, with Mr Tiffen's proposal imminent, could she afford to postpone her decline much longer? Long enough, that was, until the Mertons' ball when she might see Harry again. But what difference could it make if she did? she thought, her gloom deepening, because even making the outrageous assumption that he was overpoweringly enamoured of her, he was scarcely going to declare himself at their second meeting— especially with Mr Tiffen in attendance. Besides, she reflected, trying to view the matter more dispassionately, Harry was a pattern-card bachelor so marriage must be out of the question: which left the alternative of being offered a *carte blanche* (an expression she had learnt from her extensive reading of novels), and not even Theo, she thought unkindly, would draw such an offer from a strange gentleman in two meetings! How *she* should set about it was more than she could imagine. She was, she had decided after a lot of agitated thought, and failing all else, quite prepared to become Harry's mistress, but how did one achieve such an ambition? Particularly when it seemed out of her power even to exchange more than two words with the object of her affections without being rendered speechless with apprehension. In comparison with these insuperable wordly riddles, an unspectacular spell of malingering was clearly much to be preferred: silently she renounced her love for Harry —for the time being, in any event. She would have luncheon and then start her decline . . .

"You're uncommonly quiet, Merry, but then I expect you're a trifle worried about Mr Tiffen."

"Mr Tiffen?" echoed Almeria, not certain which particular anxiety of hers about that gentleman was being referred to.

"Yes, his wretched toothache—and it is not a simple tooth-drawing affair, I collect, but an abscess."

"Abscess?" Almeria repeated blankly, brought down to earth with a start. "Mr Tiffen has the toothache?"

"Did you not know? But then, I suppose he thought it would cast a blight over your evening if he told you. He is a gentleman of the first sensibility and consideration."

"But how did you know?"

"Well, I must own I noticed he looked a touch out of sorts, and I enquired if anything ailed him."

"Oh, dear," Almeria said, feeling very guilty. "I should have noticed, shouldn't I?"

Frances looked up from her work and smiled. "Well, I shouldn't blame yourself too much. I expect he did his best to conceal his discomfort from you. I am glad, by the by, that you seem to be on more cordial terms with each other—I noticed you sat out with him last night instead of playing cards."

Almeria did not know what answer to return to this uncomfortable speech. "I expect he'll be well enough to attend the Mertons' ball next week, won't he?" she observed at last.

"You may depend upon it, I'm sure. After all, it will be about the last dance of any note of this season, and he is bound to want to have the pleasure of escorting you there. Who knows, perhaps he will take the opportunity to propose."

Almeria felt it was time to turn the subject. "I haven't found my pearl necklace, you know."

"It must be somewhere in your room, I'll be bound. After all, you didn't lose it while you were wearing it, did you?"

"No, I'm perfectly sure of that. I'll ask Meg to look for it when next she cleans my bedchamber thoroughly."

That afternoon, Mrs Denbury received a letter from Mr Tiffen to say that he had developed a slight fever, and did not believe he would be well enough to stir out of doors for some days, and therefore they must not look to see him at the Mertons' dance. When Mrs Denbury acquainted her two daughters and Frances with the news, she added: "How tiresome it is—just when Plumptree is to be restored to us. Never mind, what a blessing that Sir Henry and the major were thrown in our way. I have secured invitations for them from Lady Merton and am confident of their acceptance. Such a dearth of gentlemen there always is at this season, they are like eggs in winter!"

To Almeria, already endeavouring to look pale and a trifle wan, this news was disconcerting to say the least of it. Ultimately she decided yet again to defer her decline, and although well aware that her prospects of captivating Harry had not been improved substantially by this stroke of fate, she began to look forward to their second meeting.

Appreciative of the fact that her thick golden hair was one of her better features (even if it was not the fashionable dark colouring of her sisters) she took the unusual step of asking Travers to put up her hair in curl-papers the night before the dance. Consequently, when she had a slight headache the following morning she put it down to the highly uncomfortable night she had passed, which had culminated in her sleeping prone, and almost suffocating. She could eat very little but ascribed that to her habitual nervous apprehension before any assembly; however, as the day progressed she felt even less enthusiastic than usual at the approach of a rout, in spite of Harry's certain presence there.

Nonetheless, she donned her velvet and lamé dress, but as she looked dizzily at her reflection the cheval mirror seemed to move. She leaned forward to put out a hand as if to steady it, and the next thing she knew she was lying on the floor. Her heart was beating wildly as if it had taken a new, alarming life of its own, and she felt too weak and frightened to move. Her eyes flickered open and dimly she saw her pearl necklace on the floor behind the dressing-table, but it was quite beyond her powers to retrieve it.

Travers, looking in on Miss Almeria to see if she required any assistance with dressing her hair, found her half-lying, half-sitting on the floor.

"Whatever's the matter, Miss? My word, you're pale. Still, it's not like you to swoon, is it? Come, let's get you to the bed." The maid, for one so deft and light-fingered with the needle, was of sturdy build and soon lifted the girl on to the bed, where she lay curled up and shivering. "Bless me, the mistress had best be told about this."

"Oh . . . no." Almeria found it took every ounce of her strength to murmur this feeble protest, and could do no more when Travers responded: "Oh, *yes*, Miss—I'll be back directly."

She drifted into a sort of limbo into which her mother's voice intruded eventually. "—I expect it is simply a ruse to avoid accompanying us tonight. Well, at least her escort is absent, too, so it does not signify a great deal on this occasion."

There was a nearby rustle of silk, a chink of a bracelet, and a cool hand was placed in a business-like fashion on Almeria's forehead.

"—Hm, no fever that I can detect."

"She is shivering, though, ma'am," Travers pointed out.

"As well she might, throwing us into a turmoil like this," Mrs Denbury retorted with the utmost calm. "Well, there is no question of crying off from my engagement tonight. Perhaps you can look in on her from time to time, Travers, and I should give her a dose of laudanum if she really does have the headache."

"You don't think the doctor should be summoned, ma'am?" Travers suggested tentatively, one eye on the huddled figure in front of them.

"Certainly not—not for a fit of the vapours. Ah, I can hear the carriage at the door, I must go." And she left, not having addressed a single word of enquiry or sympathy to her daughter.

Not that it would have made a vast amount of difference if she had, as Travers found out when she tried to question the girl herself about her condition. Any effort to speak occasioned a sob, followed by a bout of heartbroken weeping. Travers shook her head, then, baffled, rang for the housemaid to render some assistance in putting young Miss Almeria to bed.

Travers had been with the Denbury family for a greater part of Almeria's life and was not unkind, but nor was hers a demonstrative nature and she was quite at a loss to know how to comfort the girl. Mrs Denbury's brisk recommendation of a sleeping draught did seem the best remedy, and she managed to dose the trembling patient at last.

The laudanum gave Almeria very little rest, though: she tossed about and slept but fitfully and then only to be engulfed in nightmares. At some time, she had no idea when, Frances appeared before her and started to ask her how she went on. It was impossible to put her various alarming sensations into words and all she mentioned was the pain in her left side.

"Is there anything else you want to tell me?" Frances asked.

Almeria, by this time, was quite convinced she was dying but she was not in the least upset by the prospect, as she had imagined one would be: she felt so weary she welcomed the possibility and gave no thought to her family or Harry—or even Fanny, at her bedside. The only thing that seemed important was to tell Fanny about the necklace: if she didn't, it might never be found, and for some

reason this worried her more than anything else.
She tried to explain but the words wouldn't form,
so she put her hand to her neck.

"Your throat hurts?" said Frances.

Almeria shook her head, quite in despair over
this trivial matter. Her hand moved feebly and
caught at a lock of her long blonde hair.

"Oh, I see, you want to keep your hair. Don't
fret, Merry, I shan't let anyone cut it off, I promise."

Defeated, Almeria closed her eyes, and the tears
welled up under the lids . . .

Voices occasionally penetrated her sick, drugged
senses . . . Travers', her mother's, Frances' and a
gentleman's unfamiliar one.

"I confess, ma'am, it is a baffling case, but I
can recommend with the utmost confidence the
following course of treatment—Digitalis for the bad
action of the heart, Globar salts for any swimming
of the senses, and a hot poultice for the pain in the
side. But without the additional, most vital benefit
of phlebotomy, of course, the response may not be
immediate. Still, as you must know, it would not
be wise to bleed her until the moon wanes."

There was some discussion between what was
clearly the doctor and various women's indistinct
voices. Ultimately the doctor said: "Good, well I
will call daily and as soon as I can undertake the
bleeding, I will, I assure you."

Under the doctor's regimen, and with laudanum

still being used to make her sleep, Almeria showed no improvement. Various nourishing broths were fed to her but she was scarcely aware of anything but her heart, which hovered between anvil-like beats and frantic flutterings: the pain in her side persisted despite the poultices.

Once, she managed to talk to Frances. "Fanny, don't let them bleed me, will you?"

"I'll try not to. Can you tell me what's wrong, though? What is it that is upsetting you so?"

"I feel dreadful and just want to be left alone, that's all," she murmured.

Then, the doctor's voice was there again, and her mother's. Her pulse was taken, her eyes examined and her forehead felt.

"Amazing, amazing. . . . You say she's always been a sickly child, ma'am? Mm. Mm. Headaches . . . lethargy, mm, mm . . . No, no improvement whatever, I quite agree, but there's still the phlebotomy to be tried, remember."

At that point the voices went further away and Almeria could only hear occasional snatches of the doctor's ingratiating accents. "—couldn't be responsible in that event . . . very grave consequences. . . . recovery unlikely, then, and wouldn't say more than a year or two to live at best. . . . Yes, that's my considered professional opinion . . . As you wish, ma'am . . . I'll render my account in due course. Good day to you."

The words meant very little to Almeria in her

lowered drowsy state and she went to sleep once
more. Later, another doctor's voice was heard—
with elderly, gentler accents. ". . . no, just let her
rest, but cut down the laudanum gradually and
give balm, nothing else. Try to persuade her to eat,
and to talk now and then . . . No, there's no need
for me to call daily, unless there's a marked change
for the worse."

Almeria had lost all sense of time, but it was
shortly after this point that she began to feel a little
stronger and able to take notice of her surroundings again.

Mrs Denbury looked in from time to time but
Travers and Frances seemed to be in her room the
most. Frances had the task of encouraging the patient to eat, and was cheered one morning to see
Almeria awake and looking about her.

"Hallo, it's nice to see the colour of those pretty
hazel eyes again! You do look better today."

"Yes," agreed Almeria, struggling to sit up. "Oh,
I'm so weak."

"Bound to be, you've been in bed nearly two
weeks. Here, let me help you."

"Two weeks!" Almeria looked in consternation
at her cousin. "What's been wrong with me?"

"Well, that's rather hard to say as *you* couldn't
tell us anything without your breaking into tears
all the while."

"I was frightened—"

"Yes, I'm sure you were, poor love, never mind."

"—but only at first, then I didn't care. —Oh, I remember now!" The memory of the first doctor's voice came back to her: *One or two years to live.*

"What is it you remember?" Frances asked, as she prepared to give her cousin breakfast.

"Ugh—sago! Couldn't I have chocolate as I usually do?"

"That's better!" said Frances with a relieved smile. "That's the first natural reaction I've had from you for weeks. Yes, I'll ring for some and have this beastly stuff taken away." She walked across to the bell-pull. "What was it you remembered that was so unpleasant?"

"Oh, I don't know—I've forgotten," Almeria said with an evasive and shaky smile. "Are you sure the doctor hasn't put a name to whatever is wrong with me?"

"Well, I've not heard if he has, but stop worrying about it, you're going to get better now, that's all that counts. You've had no fever, haven't thrown a rash—in fact you've shown no self-respecting symptoms at all! It's your mama's opinion it was a severe crisis of nerves."

"Oh, it couldn't have been, Fanny! My heart was most shockingly affected, and that pain in my side, well, that hasn't quite eased even now."

"They were probably just palpitations you suffered, you know."

Almeria did not pursue the matter: no one was going to repeat either doctors' verdicts to her, that was obvious, and Fanny may not know about it at all.

She soon tired after her first bout of talking, and although she exchanged a few words with her mother later in the day it was not for two more days that she took an interest in anything beyond her own condition. Then, Theo came in to see her: a very subdued Theo with little to say at first, but her presence served to remind Almeria of the existence of the outside world.

"You missed a capital ball, swooning away like that, Merry," Theo informed her finally after a perfunctory enquiry about her present state of health. "Quite the best of the season, wasn't it, Fanny, not the least trace of starch. Why, we had *four* waltzes, imagine! I stood up for one of them with Sir Henry, who dances amazingly well in spite of that limp of his. Well, I had to do something to set Plumptree in his place after the shameful way he neglected me, did I not? Oh, by the by, we are getting married next month, but you'll be well by then, won't you, so you'll be able to come."

At this point Frances intervened. "I think Merry is not quite stout enough to be enthusing about dances and weddings at this present, Theo."

"Oh no, sorry," said Theo, abashed, and she fell silent again . . . "Well, I'll come and see you again tomorrow, sister."

Needless to say this brief visit threw Almeria into an agitated state: until then she had been able

THE SHY YOUNG DENBURY   113

to disregard what she now considered as her previous life, but mention of Harry, and Theo's wedding brought it all back to her. With these memories had come the spectre of Mr Tiffen and his offer.

"Fanny, what happened to Mr Tiffen? Is he well again?"

"Bless you, yes! I did mention him to you occasionally, but I think you were too insensible to comprehend what was being said. He has been in attendance here almost daily enquiring after your health. I expect he may be able to visit you for a few minutes soon; if you so wish," Frances added carefully.

"Oh, I don't think I want to see him just yet," Almeria protested, knowing that she never wanted to see him again. She must tell her mother that it was out of the question to marry him now—as she herself must know as there was only a limited span of life left to her. She could not get used to that prospect: as she grew stronger it became steadily more distressing; at first she had not cared one jot. However, she did not think she would mention it to anyone if they did not do so first. She *could* ask her mother about it, in case she had misheard, or even dreamt the whole episode (although she was certain she had not) but she would not be able to believe anything she was told. Of course, her mother would deny it, and nothing could be gained by brangling over it.

Mrs Denbury sat with her bed-ridden daughter

for almost two hours one afternoon, an action which in itself alarmed Almeria. Such solicitude she had not come to expect from her parent: she must indeed be gravely ill.

"Should you like me to read to you, Almeria?"

"No, thank you, mama!" Almeria couldn't imagine such a thing, but she was quite honest when she added she had lost interest in books for the moment.

"I could scarcely pretend I was wholly sorry to hear that, could I, not after the way I have berated you for reading." Mrs Denbury delivered this remark in tones of pleasant good nature. "But if you are to be confined to the house for some weeks, and I imagine you must be, I hope you will recover some of your bookish interest. Otherwise time is bound to hang heavy for you.

"If you feel strong enough I should like to talk to you, but I hope you may not go into tears! I know you have been like Niobe, all tears, of late but Fanny says you are much improved in that respect now. Not that I have the least desire to upset you, indeed no."

Almeria, propped up against her pillows, listened disbelievingly to these strange and soothing words from her mother. Something very drastic must have occurred to render her so amicable: it had to be the doctor's fatal verdict—she could think of no other explanation. Was she going to be prepared for the news, now? If so, she hoped she would retain her composure.

8

"May I get you anything, a drink, perhaps?" Mrs
Denbury asked Almeria as she drew up a chair by
the bedside.

"No, thank you, mama."

"Poor child, your eyes are as round as cartwheels!
Am I really such a Mormo to you? I do blame myself, I should have made more allowances for your
delicate constitution, and realised you were *different*
from my other girls. Ah well, better late than never,
I suppose, and it would soon have been too late to
remedy."

Almeria's feelings during this self-culpatory
speech may be imagined: she was tempted so say,

'yes, I heard what the doctor said, there is no need for all this hugger-mugger' but she did not. It had always been easier, with her mama, to stay silent, and out of habit she continued to do so.

"That you have been grievously ill I do not need to tell you, but I am sure your ailment had its root in what went before. I do not wish your recovery to be retarded in any way, so I want you to be quite honest with me. What are your feelings about marrying Mr Tiffen? . . . Come now, I shall offer no reproaches whatever you say."

Almeria could not believe her ears. "I don't wish to marry him, mama, or—or anyone else, ever," she said with quiet desperation.

"There's no call to add such a sweeping qualification—I shall not attempt to press you into another unwelcome match, I promise you! But, I thought I was in the right of it. Fanny had the notion you did not find the prospect of marriage with Tiffen wholly unacceptable, but she doesn't know you as I do. Oh, I daresay that does sound odd coming from my lips, but I wished to turn a blind eye to your feelings—it was not that I was unaware of them. I cannot compensate for having brought you to this low ebb but I am sorry, my dear, truly I am . . . Oh, there now, I have reduced you to tears, after all!"

Almeria produced her ever-present handkerchief and dabbed at her eyes. "No, no, mama, it's all right, really," she said in strangled tones.

"You mustn't lay blame on your papa for any of

this. He set no obstacle in Tiffen's way when he was approached on the matter, but I was the one who encouraged the match from the beginning. It was sheer selfishness on my part, I see that now. I really could not face the prospect of another season acting chaperon and entertaining a host of people one has nothing but contempt for, in truth. I had much rather have a snug dinner and card-party, as you know. I was aware," she said more thoughtfully, "that the constant round of entertainments was a cruel strain on *your* nerves—and then the peremptory betrothal clearly dealt a killing blow to your tender young system. But no, there shall be no excuses. I was in error and I freely confess it." She saw that Almeria had regained a measure of tranquillity. "Am I not right in my estimation of your sentiments on the matter?"

"Yes, mama." Almeria had not seen her situation quite in this light before, and she did think perhaps the reason for her collapse and subsequent prostration might be contained in this thesis. "I should not wish to endure another season, on any account," she said with a watery smile.

"And nor shall you, my dear! We will both withdraw from the lists!" She got to her feet and shook out the elaborate flouncings of her ruby merino dress. "I shan't weary you further— I have, I hope, relieved your mind of its prime anxiety, so you may sleep more peacefully, perhaps. You must husband your strength and try to banish those dark circles from beneath your eyes."

"Shall you tell Mr Tiffen of my decision? What will you say?"

"Your papa will attend to that," Mrs Denbury said firmly. "I expect he will ascribe it to the uncertain state of your health. Mr Tiffen may still call upon us from time to time, I hope, for he is to officiate at Theo's wedding, but there will be a lapse of time before you need encounter him again, and I trust any awkwardness attendant upon the situation may have dissipated by then. Now, try to rest, my dear." She laid a hand briefly on Almeria's arm before she left.

Almeria did not sleep but remained staring into space for some time . . .

It was a judgement, she concluded eventually, for planning to escape from her marriage by simulated illness: the scheme had succeeded with a vengeance, but the illness was real and brought a sentence of death with it. Nothing that her mother had said removed the fear of that from her mind, and indeed her whole attitude to her daughter had undergone such a severe reversal that, in Almeria's opinion, only something of a most drastic nature could account for it.

Almeria was still in the same position when Frances came in with a tray.

"You have certainly chosen the right time of year to be recruiting your strength! Here is partridge— sent up for you by the Mertons from their country establishment, melon brought by Major Maunby and some Morello cherries from Mr Tiffen. Cook has devised all manner of tempting dishes for you, and appears to be making it her personal responsibility to restore you to health single-handed!" Frances chattered, and Almeria noticed, not without some envy, her eyes were bright and her complexion glowing.

"Yes, it looks much too good to eat. How kind everyone is! I had not realised my indisposition was so well known abroad. Major Maunby brought the melon, you say? Himself? Or was it carried by a servant?"

"No, he gave it into your mama's care with his very own hand," Frances said playfully. "He—he has been calling with some frequency of late—you see, I go riding with him sometimes. He would have preferred, I think, to take me driving but he has no carriage in town, so I proposed we should ride instead. We are so near the country here, and have had some delightful excursions—I didn't want to mention it to you before, in case it should make you feel all the more wretched being cooped up indoors!"

"How foolish of you! You must think me a perfect dog-in-the-manger! I'm very pleased you have had some diversion whilst you've been at my beck and call." Almeria sampled the partridge. "Delicious . . . I didn't know you had a riding-dress— or a horse, for that matter."

"Nor have I, I haven't ridden since—oh, for

some years," she said hastily. "But Major Maunby
has provided for me."

"Not the riding-dress, I trust?" put in Almeria,
with a glimmer of her old spirit.

"Of course not, how could you say so! No, he
has hired for me a most sedate dapple-grey, and I
have rashly purchased a riding-dress of the prettiest
shade of blue."

"You must present a lovely picture—I should
like to see you." Though she couldn't imagine being
part of an outdoor scene again.

"Well, since you know all about it now, I will
come in to you before I set out the next time. Oh,
and by the by, I should have told you before, your
pearl necklace was discovered behind the dressing-
table—Meg did find it."

Almeria gave an odd little laugh. "I had quite
forgotten it again. I saw it, you know, when I fell
that night—I tried to tell you, but couldn't."

Frances stared at her. "When *I* thought you were
telling me about your hair! I'm sorry, I never
guessed—"

"Why should you? It wasn't important—it just
seemed so to me at the time."

"Better you should have kept your lovely hair!"

"That's not very important, either, I shan't be
going into society again."

"You mustn't say so! Oh, I have just seen your
mama and she told me about your crying off from
Mr Tiffen. You are perfectly certain about that,

are you?" she asked, looking at her cousin very earnestly.

"Of course, I am! I cannot abide Mr Tiffen, you must know that!"

"Well no, I didn't, I rather thought—but there, I am glad you have resolved the matter. Yes, very glad," she added with a genuinely pleased smile.

The next day the doctor called. Almeria felt able to take notice of him this time, and saw that he was a white-haired gentleman, of small stature and gentle mien but with surprising, lively blue eyes. She observed also that he had a look of salubrity about him, always reassuring in a physician.

"There, what did I tell you, Mrs Denbury? Soon be as right as ninepence, won't we?" He grasped Almeria's wrist in an amazingly warm hand and his dancing eyes were still for a moment as they fixed upon the dial of his pocket watch. "Good, nothing amiss there," he pronounced at last.

"Oh, but it still beats awfully fast sometimes, in the most alarming fashion," Almeria told him quickly.

"Sure to, for a time, my dear, nothing to worry about at all! You'll find it races and rattles a bit when you get up—which you're going to do from today—but it doesn't signify, no, not in the least. Valerian she shall have, Ma'am," he said, his eyes darting to Mrs Denbury. "I'll let you have the receipt."

"You think I *will* get better, then, sir?" Almeria made herself ask.

"Better? Why, you're better already, child! Oh, it will seem a slow business returning wholly to your accustomed state, and you're bound to have a fit of the megrims from time to time, but you will, you will—patience! Plenty of nourishing food—which I'm sure you do not lack with Mrs Manners as cook." Here he shot a winking glance at Mrs Denbury again. "—And a little gentle exercise as soon as maybe. A short perambulation daily perhaps, before the autumn days shorten, eh?"

"What about the fixed pain at my side?" Almeria persisted.

"That will fade, depend upon it. It's not so acute as it was, is it?"

"Well, no," she admitted.

"There you are, then!" He turned to Mrs Denbury with a smile. "Well, ma'am, if you'll excuse me, I must be away to visit someone who *really* needs my services," he concluded in a teasing voice.

Almeria had several more pressing questions she wished to put to him but the opportunity was lost; the doctor left with her mother, and she imagined him now telling her the true state of affairs about her daughter.

On early reflection she found the visit reassuring—he was so cheerful, so very encouraging—but later she came to think that his sanguine manner was just what one would expect if a fatal illness was being glossed over and the patient deceived. He was certainly a very comforting physician, but was the first blunt outspoken doctor the honest one of the pair? She had no further chance to quiz him about her various anxieties because her mother informed her later he would not be calling upon her again.

"He does not suppose a further visit would serve any useful purpose," Mrs Denbury said, when pressed for a reason for his curtailed visits; a reply which unfortunately was open to misconstruction by her daughter.

Almeria felt she had been abandoned to her fate; she did, however, continue to feel stronger and her spirits inevitably improved as she was able to leave her bed and dress for an increasing period each day.

"What a blessing you bought these delightful new gowns!" Frances exclaimed one morning. A remark which was followed by an awkward silence from both ladies: Frances supposed the purchases to have been made with a marriage in mind, which had now faltered; Almeria knew they had been made with a sham illness in mind, which had succeeded only too well.

"Yes, I am particularly fond of this pink sarcenet," Almeria managed to say at last, in casual tones. "Are you riding with the major today, Fanny?"

"I expect so, this afternoon."

Fanny had been in such glowing good looks of late, Almeria was convinced she was in love with Major Maunby. She decided to do a little probing. "I did not meet the major above once, but he seemed all that was pleasant. Is he permanently fixed in London?"

"I'm not sure he is, for he lodges with Sir Henry Chirton—the gentleman he accompanied here on their first visit."

"Yes, I remember him," said Almeria, her heart thrown into palpitations of a different sort than usual.

"The major is a frustrated soldier, I fear, placed on half-pay and fretting for battle. He reminds me, in so many ways, of—well, never mind that . . . I believe his home is in Berkshire. He is the youngest of three sons of an earl, and I fancy he feels rather *de trop* there, poor man. Sir Henry, too, was a captain in the army, but sold out after being quite severely injured at Salamanca. He has made a remarkable recovery to be left only with such a slight limp. He is from home at the moment, it seems— called away into the country on some business matter. Oh, but it was the major you were enquiring after, was it not?"

But Almeria made sure of furthering her sparse knowledge of Harry, all the same. "Where does he live?"

"Not very far away—in Soho Square. Quite the grandest house, you may imagine! Major Maunby and I rode past it one day and he would like to have shown me over it, I fancy, but it would not be the thing at all, of course—such a bachelor establishment! I do not believe Sir Henry has a lady to do any entertaining for him. In fact, he seems to be rather alone in the world, his parents both died when he was quite young, I am told." This compassionate speech conjured up a pitiful, deprived orphan in Almeria's mind, difficult to reconcile with the buoyant Harry she knew. "I am perfectly sure, though, he has remained unmarried by inclination rather than lack of opportunity—according to Major Maunby half the ladies in London have laid siege to Harry, as he calls him."

This remark revealed to Almeria how near her secret was to being discovered; if Major Maunby referred just once to Old Harry Frances might well recall her disclosure about a gentleman of that name. Almeria changed the subject hastily.

"I was thinking of asking mama if I could have a dog," she announced, a little wildly: the idea had re-occurred to her recently, but parental opposition to such a step had been total in the past.

"Why, I think that's a splendid idea! It would be company for us on our 'perambulations', and which incidentally I think we should commence any day —I am sure you are strong enough now."

"Not until next week perhaps, when the weather might be drier," Almeria temporized; she was a trifle apprehensive of her first excursion outdoors.

"You know papa would never countenance a lap-dog, as he calls them all, in the house," she said, reverting to the earlier subject. "He thinks a dog should earn its keep, and would as lief sanction a pack of fox-hounds as one pet dog. Not that I would care greatly for some lap dogs myself—do you remember in that novel we read earlier this year . . . *Mansfield Park,* Lady somebody-or-other had a pug, and a sluggish beast it sounded, too!"

"Lady Bertram," supplied Frances. "She was the sluggish one, if I recall aright!"

"Yes, perhaps even pug would have relished *some* exercise between the sweetmeats!"

"What sort of dog does take your fancy?"

"There's scant point in discussing that, Fanny, you know as well as I do it wouldn't be permitted."

Two days later brought a visit from Almeria's married sister, Mrs Charles Vine. It was Cordelia's first call upon her sick sister although she lived in Golden Square scarcely ten minutes' drive away.

"Merry, my dear sister!" she cried, advancing towards her with her black-and-white spaniel held on a leash in one hand. "I am pleased to see you go on so well. Look, I have brought you a present!" She handed the leash to Almeria who stared in bewilderment.

"But she's your dog, Cordelia."

"Yes, she is—or was—and I love her dearly, but you see the case is this," she hesitated and blushed becomingly under her fashionable, high-crowned bonnet, "we are *both* increasing and Mr Vine says one of us must go! Well, I was greatly upset at first, as you may imagine, but when papa said *you* wanted a dog and asked where I had procured mine—well, it seemed a perfect solution, so here she is!"

"Papa said?" Almeria repeated, looking up wonderingly from stroking the spaniel.

"Why yes, I was a trifle taken aback, I own, for I know how *adamant* he was used to be on the matter, but it seems he's mellowed with the years! Well, aren't you going to congratulate me?" she said with a pout.

"I'm sorry, I'm a little overwhelmed by all of this! Of course, I congratulate you, Cordelia, I'm delighted!"

"When is it to be?" asked Frances, who had been watching this exchange with a satisfied smile.

"Not until next March."

"I must stitch some baby-linen for you, whatever you wish—I shall have plenty of time," Almeria said somewhat ruefully.

"Mama is making me a list of all I shall need— it seems quite endless! I'll let you know the next time I call."

"Thank you so much for entrusting—oh, dear, I've quite forgotten your name," Almeria told the spaniel who had settled contentedly at her feet, unaware of the momentous event about to befall her.

"It's *Hecuba,* I fear," Cordelia responded. "Mr Vine chose it, you know, and he is of a classical turn of mind. I call her Hec when he's not within earshot—that seems to serve very well," she giggled.

"Well, he's not within earshot here, so Hec it is! Thank you, anyway, you may rest assured she will have every attention—Oh, I'd forgotten, you said *she* was increasing, too! Papa cannot know that!"

"Oh yes, I should have landed in the suds if I had omitted to disclose that vital fact!"

"And he didn't object?" Almeria asked, stunned.

"No, not so much as a demur."

"Well . . ." said Almeria, anything more comprehensive being beyond her.

"Her litter is due next month, about the third week."

"I don't know anything about rearing puppies," Almeria declared, with a worried frown.

"I daresay Hec will manage, won't you, love?" Cordelia nudged the somnolent spaniel's muzzle with the toe of her kid boot. "I don't know a vast amount about rearing babies, either!"

"Yes, but you will have a nurse—I shall be Hec's nurse!" Almeria retorted.

"We'll manage between the three of us, I fancy," Frances said in reassuring tones.

Provision for Hecuba's well-being seemed to shorten the days for Almeria because, besides precipitating her daily walk, she had to consult with Mrs Manners about the food to be sent up for her, and to groom the dog's silky coat regularly. Mrs

Denbury had deliberately left her daughter in sole charge of the animal to prevent her brooding over her own lowered condition.

It was a scheme which worked very well, except when Almeria lay in bed trying to sleep: then restlessness would overtake her, her palpitations often ensued, and she became convinced she had only a limited span ahead of her. As the weeks passed and her strength and natural resilience returned, she was still not able to disregard the dire prophecy of the original doctor but she did face the prospect with more resolution.

After all, she told herself, anyone could be struck down without warning with smallpox, cholera, the consumption and a host of other plagues: why even Cordelia, whom she had congratulated so warmly, faced a considerable risk in childbed; but she had had a warning and it was up to her to make the best she could of what time was left to her. Two years was still quite a long time, she reflected staunchly, taking the maximum span allotted to her: and it was clear she was not going to be wholly infirm throughout that time—indeed, sometimes she felt quite like her old self. The upshot of her lengthy reflections was that she would try to conduct her life in her accustomed fashion—but there would be one benefit which would accrue from the threat which hung over her: she had not the least intention of being the Shy Young Denbury any longer.

For what had she to lose now by her behaviour, however outrageous?

Her principal ambition was unchanged by her illness: she would fix Harry's interest somehow, but would no longer be impeded by her old shrinking nature, or by social convention.

She started to make her plans, and soon realised it was not going to be easy. To begin with, she had not the smallest desire to break Harry's heart; although it was not as if she were bent on becoming his wife. Gentlemen, she knew from her vast consumption of novels, were always discarding mistresses, so her loss after a year or two need not deal him too devastating a blow. Persuading him that a well-bred girl like herself was willing to be his mistress might well present the greatest difficulty, she surmised: but she would cross that particular bridge when she came to it—and she might not come to it for some little time, considering the tenuous state of their present relationship.

But, she was not daunted—she would concentrate on devising her first assault on Harry's defences, as soon as he should return to his town house.

9

Harry, unaware that a replacement was imminent, was seriously contemplating discarding Rosa Bezzolini, his mistress of the past two years.

It was November: a gloomy time of year, especially in the deserted town, and calculated to promote introspection, although that was not, in Harry's case, the prime cause of his present mopish reflections. The fact was that the unexpected death of his godfather, Hubert Jasper Parfitt, seemed to have cast him into a state of inquietude and dissatisfaction with his own mode of life: he could not claim that Parfitt's death in itself had caused him

to suffer any great affliction. He had not seen the
gentleman, an old rakehelly friend of his father's,
for some years: not since he had turned his attentions from the London scene and inflicted his
disturbing presence on the neighbourhood of Scarborough. It seemed an unlikely place for a loose-
fish to gravitate ('Hubert Parfitt, far from perfect'
was the opening line of a ribald verse, which Harry
could recall circulating some years ago in the Clubs,
before the gentleman departed for the Northern
fastness); however, he had owned a house not far
from the spa town and had evidently decided his
dissolute style of life could be sustained a little less
expensively there, than in the metropolis. He had,
amongst his other wild pursuits, been a hard rider
to hounds and typically had broken his neck, out
of season, exercising his own pack in solitary style:
the fatal outcome was not altogether a surprise to
those about him as he had consumed four bottles
of port before he set out, and the horse had im-
bibed one as well.

It had, however, been a complete surprise to
Harry to learn that he was the sole beneficiary of
Hubert Parfitt's estate: the only connexion between
godfather and godson hitherto had been the sharing of the name Jasper; indeed, that was the only
connexion Harry's mother had desired as she had
regarded the sponsorship as disastrous from the
outset. Harry's father had died when he was only
twelve and his sister fifteen, but his mother had

reared them both without recourse to Parfitt's aid, and when she followed her husband in '03, Harry had promptly shut up their house in Soho Square and bought a pair of colours for himself—he was then eighteen. His sister, Amy, although one-and-twenty by then, had been put into the care of god-parents of her own of unimpeachable morals and character; and three years later she had married a gentleman equally dull.

Harry had travelled to Scarborough to inspect his inheritance and soon discovered that the late owner of Scantleby Hall was unlamented, except by his gambling and hunting cronies and the bawdy house abbesses of the district, and of course by his servants. He found he was the object of very hard scrutiny by the inhabitants and neighbours of the Hall, who clearly wondered what sort of a reprobate fellow had been the apple of Parfitt's eye. This had given Harry pause to think and examine his ways, and he had decided that on the face of it the critics could be pardoned for thinking he was in the way of being a worthy successor to Hubert Parfitt. It was not so, of course, he was no rakeshame of Parfitt's class; but would he be so, by the time he was Parfitt's age?

These introspective thoughts had been constantly at the back of his mind as he inspected the Scantleby estate—which included a most elegant Palladian residence, in a state of abominable neglect and decay. He had imagined the Hall would be a mean stone dwelling with little style and less comfort, as he had never penetrated the wilds of Yorkshire before, but Hubert Parfitt had lived in a degree of style, and even comfort in his own wing: but beyond that Harry surmised that not a repair had been made since the house was built in the early eighteenth century. However it was not too late to restore the building to its original glories, and it was set in a piece of pretty parkland—but again in a state of sad neglect.

Certainly the house interested Harry, and he was disinclined to put it on the market right away as Parfitt's lawyer seemed to expect he would: but he was also disinclined to follow in Parfitt's footsteps as the notorious bachelor owner of Scantleby Hall. He had stayed at the local inn for some two weeks, had dismissed some of the Scantleby servants and retained others, and had charged the lawyer, a Scarborough man, to seek out a reliable fellow who could supervise some essential repairs to the house before the onset of the ravages of another east coast winter.

In a highly uncertain and dissatisfied frame of mind he had set out to return to London. His dissatisfaction had not been lessened by an additional country visit he had made on his way back to town. Deciding he had been somewhat lax in his fraternal duties since his return from the Peninsula war, having paid only one previous visit to his sister in the last three years, he called upon Amy and her dreary husband in Derbyshire. Only for the second time did he make the acquaintance of his two nieces and one nephew, the latter being now five years old.

He had later expressed some of his discontent with what he had found, to Crispin on his return home.

"As things stand at present the boy is my heir," Harry explained, "and frankly the idea appals me. A more disagreeable bratling I have rarely seen."

"Dammit, Harry," protested Crispin, "five is a trifle young to judge the poor mite's character, isn't it? Why at that tender age I was the most terrible rapscallion up to no end of bobbery, and look at me now!"

"Exactly! No discernible change whatever! Proved my point if I may say so," Harry said, grinning. "But a bit of spirit I've never minded in a young'un but this little fellow looks set to reform the world! Never saw him laugh once, and wanted to engage me in earnest discussion on Mr Locke's *Essay Concerning Human Understanding* when I enquired kindly what fairy tale he was reading!"

Crispin roared. "At five! No, you're bamming me, I'll not believe it!"

"It's the sober truth—I'd not jest about such a dire matter, I do assure you. The devil of it is my sister named him Henry—a matter of equal regret to us both, I fancy. If he'd as much as pinched his sisters once, I'd have thought there might be a ray of hope—and it would have done *them* no harm to be tweaked into life, I may tell you! Amy was clearly relieved when their contaminating uncle departed! She has always disapproved strongly of my ramshackle ways and is determined such characteristics shall not mar her offspring."

"I'd say she was going the best way about ensuring they do play the devil sooner or later."

"Ay, and nothing could be more disastrous than that—a rare kick-up there'll be, and young Henry will make Hubert Parfitt look pale by comparison, I daresay. On the other hand, he might stay exactly the way he is," he said in gloomy tones, "and when he succeeds to my fortune no doubt found a college for fire-eating philosophers at Scantleby Hall with it. It won't do, you must see that!"

"Oh, I do! Your sister might produce further heirs, of course, but—" Crispin was saying thoughtfully when Harry cut across him in anguished tones.

"She is, she is, in the spring! They're mighty proud of their prodigies and won't be satisfied till they have a quiverful, but they'll all be cast in the same mould so what's the gain?"

"Considerable, I would say, for the College of Philosophers unless you do something about it," retorted Crispin.

"Yes," said Harry at last, "my conclusion, precisely."

"Soberin', ain't it, but it seems we all have to face it in the end."

"Hubert Parfitt didn't," Harry observed.

"No, but he was a loose screw if ever there was one—if half your tales of him are true! You can't want to tread in his footsteps."

"I don't," said Harry shortly.

"Well then, join me on the road to parson's mousetrap!" Crispin exhorted him, in bracing tones.

"*Are* you on the road to parson's mousetrap?" Harry asked, swiftly turning the tables on him.

Crispin favoured his friend with a wonderfully innocent blue-eyed gaze. "It's not New Year's Eve, is it?"

"Very well, you old rogue, keep your secrets. Although it is no secret, I collect, that you have been much in the company of Mrs Wren whilst I've been away?" Harry knew, of course, that the dapple-grey, kept in his stables, was Mrs Wren's mount.

"No, none," he said succinctly, then added after a pause, "By the by, I shall be going into Berkshire in the next week or so for a space."

This studiedly casual remark drew a non-committal 'Oh' from Harry and no more.

"Yes, thought it was time I faced the family, y'know—and got in a bit of shooting," he explained in artless tones.

"Oh, quite," agreed Harry, straight-faced. Since the last time they had discussed this matter Crispin would not go next nor nigh the ancestral home because of Meg Venables, Harry presumed this turn-about must mean that Cris was tolerably sure of marrying someone else—Mrs Wren?—and wanted his family's approval to seal the match. However, all he said was: "You'll be riding, I collect? Well then, you must take Minstrel to carry you."

Crispin demurred about this offer only briefly: he'd had no saddle-horse of his own in town and had ridden Harry's mare, Minstrel, since he had moved into Soho Square.

It did appear, Harry thought later, that events seemed to be inexorably nudging him into matrimony. His best friend on the way to being leg-shackled (against all the odds, too!), an empty country house crying out for a family to be raised in it, and his only heir a sore disappointment, to put it at its very mildest. There was Rosa Bezzolini, as well, where his dejected thoughts had originated that darkling November afternoon.

His mistress was a young Italian dancer—much younger in fact than he had known when he selected her from the dancers in the pink room behind the Opera House stage. He had judged her to be eighteen—a sloe-eyed Latin beauty with not one word of English at her command—but when he had, over the ensuing months, painstakingly taught her his native language he discovered she was barely seventeen, even then. He had established her in an apartment near the Haymarket, and to begin with she had been, understandably, his devoted slave; but as she improved her English and, as a consequence, widened her acquaintance, she became less dependent upon him. He had never expected to teach her the meaning of the word constancy in any language, and was tolerably certain there were plenty of contenders willing to pay her rent when his lease on the apartment ran its course at the end of the year. All in all, Harry decided, it was time to call a halt to the relationship . . .

Finding the prospect of domesticity which seemed to be looming before him far from inspiriting, and having little idea how he should find a tolerable wife now, as he had not succeeded in doing so hitherto, he sighed despondently. The hare-brained scheme he had produced so blithely for Crispin's search for a wife, although against every expectation evidently successful, did not make a great appeal to its creator. He pondered over the idea of retiring into Yorkshire and settling at Scantleby Hall with a view to taking a local lady as wife, but came quickly to the conclusion that it might be years before a new bachelor owner of the Hall was accepted into the close-knit ranks of a provincial society. So, his search had perforce to begin in the town, but a town at present almost bereft of any fashionable society: not that he had ever found a fashionable female in the slightest degree interesting . . .

He poured the last of his wine into the glass. At that moment Tobin came in to light the candles and frowned at the quantity of wine his master had consumed that afternoon: he hoped devoutly Sir Henry would soon shake off this fit of the megrims which seemed to have afflicted him since his return from Yorkshire.

In Bedford Square October had been a comparatively eventful month: Theo's marriage to George Plumptree happened to coincide with the date Hecuba's pups were due. As it would have strained even Mr Denbury's newfound canine tolerance if a litter of pups had been delivered in the Egyptian drawing-room during the marriage ceremony, Hec had to have every restraint imposed upon her to keep her away from a closet in that apartment, which particularly took her fancy for the making of a nest. The dog had turned up her nose at an almost identical closet in the morning-room on the ground floor, but on the morning of the wedding, when Hec went ominously off her food, Almeria was compelled to lock her in the morning-room and hope for the best.

At two o'clock Theo was escorted from her bedroom by her father to the drawing-room, where Mr Plumptree, members of both families and Mr Tiffen, impressive in his clerical garb, awaited them. The bride looked splendid in blonde lace over cream satin, with a cottage bonnet of lace with ostrich feathers; the bridegroom was more colourful and almost as splendid, clad in a blue coat with long tails and gold buttons, a white swansdown waistcoat, buff breeches, white silk stockings, and the most exquisitely wrought neck-cloth that Almeria had ever seen, with the notable exception of Harry's cravats. To her relief Mr Tiffen proceeded through the ceremony with no more than the occasional stammer. It was, in fact, the first time she had seen him since her illness: he had been into Hampshire at the beginning of the month to inspect his parsonage, the glowing details of which had been retailed to her by Fanny. She was still more than willing, however, that the management of this desirable establishment should fall to some other lady's care.

Throughout the service Almeria's nerves were taut as she listened for Hec's anguished squeals from the direction of the morning-room, but no untoward sound marred the solemnity of the occasion. Fanny, Almeria noticed, was the most overcome of the party, dabbing at her eyes from time to time. Mrs Denbury withstood the assault on her emotions without a blink; merely an expression of calm satisfaction.

Presently the toasts and felicitations commenced and the imposing bride-cake was cut. With all eyes upon the bridal pair Almeria did not find the gathering—her first real appearance in society since her malady—a strain, and was able to put into practise her new resolve to be more sociable, and to take a greater interest in her fellow beings than she had done hitherto. Certainly her recent unhappy experience had rendered her less conscious and more at ease in company, with the knowledge always at the back of her mind that she need not worry about what anyone thought of her. She even succeeded in taking a very young Plumptree sister under her wing and coaxed her out of her reticence.

Consequently, it seemed to her that in no time at all the newly-wed pair had to depart to begin their journey to Richmond before the early autumn darkness fell. Their riverside house was ready to receive them: indeed, it had transpired that Mr Plumptree's brief neglect of his betrothed had not been due entirely to his horses' distemper but to a pressing need for him to supervise the finishing touches to the house. Mrs Denbury and Theo had toured it only a week before the wedding and declared it all that was wonderful. The despised connexion with the cotton manufactory seemed to have paid dividends in the form of curtains and draperies of surpassing magnificence.

Theo reappeared briefly in her travelling pelisse of amber velvet with ermine trimming and muff, and she and her husband were soon gone after a lively leave-taking of the two families. To her surprise Almeria felt quite a sense of loss; she had never been very close to either of her boisterous sisters but now that both of them had flown the nest the Bedford Square house would seem oppressively quiet without them.

It was late evening by the time Almeria could escape and see what had befallen Hecuba in the morning-room. She went in somewhat nervously, her candle held high. She found herself immediately entangled underfoot with pages of newspapers. "Hec, where are you?" Hesitating for a moment but at last discerning a squeaking noise, she went to the open door of the closet and there was the spaniel with two pups in a sea of *Morning Posts* and *Chronicles*. Relieved that the event was safely over, and also that the damage was so negligible, (her father, luckily, was too preoccupied at the moment to worry about his daily newspapers) she went in search of Fanny to tell her the good news.

The next week or so was inevitably taken up with the new arrivals: mostly in protecting them from the curiosity of all the servants and every caller to the house—amongst the latter were numbered Major Maunby and Mr Tiffen, both of whom seemed to occupy a good deal of Fanny's time.

Almeria had not forgotten her intention to captivate Harry, of course, and took a constant interest in any information which his friend, the major, might inadvertently supply. In this manner she learned that Harry was back from the North, and that Major Maunby himself was due to go into the country soon. This seemed to present an ideal opportunity to Almeria, who had decided to beard the lion in his den, as it were. She must see Harry alone somehow, and even if she waited until he should call upon them at Bedford Square again, which he might, the chances of seeing him on his own were slender. Consequently, Soho Square it had to be: it was not the thing, of course, for a lady to call unaccompanied upon a gentleman, but she swept such nice considerations aside in her new-discovered freedom.

She laid her plans and waited her chance: it came, almost too soon for her comfort. Her mother and Fanny, now that the wedding was safely in the past, had decided upon an orgy of dyeing—muslin and silk gowns, spencers and ribbons, all awaited transformation. Enveloped in aprons belonging to Mrs Manners they spent the morning, below stairs, up to their elbows in soap suds, blue and starch. In the afternoon, when Almeria announced she thought she would call upon her sister Cordelia to see how she did, she found they had progressed to ironing on the floor. It was exhausting work and Almeria was not judged to be sufficiently recovered to participate.

Mrs. Denbury looked up from her task, hair dishevelled under a decidedly crooked cap and quite unrecognisable to any of her fashionable acquaintance. "Yes, my dear, I think that is a splendid idea. Take the carriage. Oh—but we do really need Meg here to help us, don't we? And Travers is out searching for a particular dye I want."

This was exactly what she had hoped her mama would say, but would she let her go without a maid? "I shall be in a closed carriage, mama, with Bill-coachman and the groom to accompany me, and it's not above a ten-minute drive to Golden Square, is it?" she said in wheedling tones.

Her mother smiled in a distracted way as Meg handed her a hot iron and took away the cool one. "Yes, very well . . . Tell Cordelia I shall be calling upon her myself in a day or two. Oh, and you must take her some of Mrs Manners' fresh-made brawn. It seems she has developed a craving for it although I recall she was always rather partial to it! Be careful in the cold east wind, Almeria."

"Yes, mama," she said meekly, and took the brawn from the cook with hands which were inclined to shake a little. Not that she felt in any degree ill or weak now, but she realised she could be face to face with Harry within the hour, and she had not the least notion what she would say to him.

She summoned the carriage at once, and was delayed only whilst the horses were put to. All she did before she left was to provide herself with a blank sheet of paper, folded and wafered, which she directed to Sir Henry Chirton, Bt. This was to be her excuse (or one of them) for approaching his house. It would have suited her purpose, too, if Hec could have accompanied her but the pups were not old enough to be left.

She gave the basket with the pots of brawn into the groom's care, and instructed the coachman to stop at Soho Square first as there was a letter she must deliver. They seemed to arrive alarmingly soon and the carriage stopped; the groom put his head in the door, and said, "Which house is it, Miss? I'll take the letter for you."

"No!" she cried with great violence (how difficult everything was!) "I mean, no thank you, I must deliver it myself—there might be a confidential reply," she improvised, "and anyway I should like a little exercise."

"I'll accompany you."

"No!" she said again with even greater agitation, as she stepped out on to the flagway. "Really, there is no call to. I had rather go on my own." She gave him her most winning smile, and then called up to the coachman: "I may be gone some few minutes, do you tool the horses in this sharp wind."

Bill-coachman's cold-reddened face looked down at her a bit doubtfully; it wasn't like Miss Almeria to tell him how to manage his horses. "But you'll not be many minutes, will you, Miss? If you'll tell me which house 'tis, I'll take you there anyhow."

It was now or never. "No, there's not the least need. I cannot say how long I shall be—perhaps half an hour." She turned on her heel and walked away quickly, hoping they would do her bidding.

She had no idea which house was Harry's and she kept her head held high looking at numbers, whilst her hands clutched the 'note' inside her chinchilla muff. At last the right number was approaching, although by this time she had walked three-quarters of the way round the square to get to it. She couldn't hear the carriage following her, which was a relief. Without allowing herself a pause for thought, which she knew would be quite fatal to her resolution, she mounted the steps and rang the bell.

. A small slight man answered, with a narrow-cheeked face and a prominent dimple in his chin. She was not sure whether she imagined the surprise in his pale bright eyes or not. In any event he did not look too top-lofty as she had feared. In a bachelor establishment such as this one it was necessary no doubt to have servants who would disregard all kinds of untoward proceedings. "Is your master at home?" she asked, very uncertain of the best way to gain admittance.

He regarded her in a puzzled manner, unable to place her at all. "Which gentleman were you desirous of seeing, ma'am?"

He made it sound as iniquitous as she felt it was! "S-sir Henry Chirton, if you please."

"I can ascertain for you, ma'am." He gave an involuntary glance over his shoulder, then added, reluctantly it seemed: "Come in, ma'am."

She stepped over the threshold with a real sense of achievement at having advanced so far in such a dubious matter.

She looked quickly about her, but at once she heard Harry's voice in the distance: so he was home! And engaged in earnest conversation with a lady, she discovered, by listening a few moments longer.

"What name shall I say, ma'am?" The servant appeared to be deriving some secret amusement from the situation now: his eyes positively twinkled as he waited her answer.

From this point she had to improvise wildly and

to decide whether or not to divulge her real name. As it seemed in the highest degree unlikely that Harry would see her in the circumstances, she made up her mind to remain incognito for the moment. "Well, you see, the case is this," she blurted out, putting one of her various alternative plans into operation, "I was this minute walking my dog round the square and suddenly she just seemed to disappear from sight." She was overwrought enough to add weight to the story. "I am perfectly certain she slipped into your area through the railing." Her story dried up abruptly at this point for two reasons: the first one being that in her haste she had not thought to notice if there *was* an area before the house, and secondly, she realised there was an inherent weakness in this story now as she had already asked to see Harry by name!

The manservant eyed her rather oddly, and not without reason, she thought: what could she say if there wasn't an area! He became noticeably more distant and severe in his approach.

"What manner of animal is it, ma'am?"

"Oh, a black and white spaniel."

"I see . . . Well, I will make enquiries below. There is, of course, no call to disturb my master on a trivial errand of this sort," he added, probably assuming she was a neighbour he had not encountered before.

There was clearly no need to trouble Harry, she saw that only too well now, but at least it would be an explanation of a kind if Harry should suddenly emerge into the hall. However it soon became very obvious to her that that was the last thing he was likely to do. The voices were really quite clear, as the door was not quite closed.

"Heavens, what do you mean?" was the first remark she managed to discern, and this was delivered in most indignant female tones, but with a distinctly foreign accent.

"Pray, what do you think I mean?" That was Harry, no doubt of it: she hadn't realised before what a powerful voice he had.

"You may as well tell me," came the arch reply.

"No, that would make you blush," was Harry's roguish response.

"Why, do you intend to make me blush?" demanded the foreign lady, who sounded very youthful.

"I can't tell that," Harry said, in a tone which certainly made Almeria blush. "But if I do, it shall be in the dark."

"Oh Heavens, I would not be in the dark with you for all the world!"

Almeria quelled an instinct to go and shut the door at this point so that she should hear no more: what was she eavesdropping upon? It sounded like a scene of seduction, putting it at its best.

The girl's voice was heard again. "Oh Lord, are you mad . . . . ?" The next few words were lost to Almeria, but as the servant reappeared, Harry's voice suddenly boomed across the hall (or so it

seemed to the monstrously embarrassed visitor)
"Come into the closet, madame—"

The rest of that request was mercifully drowned
by the manservant, who seemed quite unmoved by
the dialogue; but then he had not heard what went
before!

"I regret, ma'am, that we can find no trace of
your spaniel."

"What was that?" She put up a hand to her fiery
cheek in a nervous gesture, and looked at him
blankly. "Oh—the spaniel, yes, thank you, thank
you."

"Nay, never pull, for I will not go!" came the
spirited declaration from the lady, who was evidently making a valiant fight for her honour.

Almeria, never more aware of the fact that she
was sadly lacking in the ways of the world, had not
the least notion how to go on: she felt vaguely that
the servant should burst in and protect the lady,
whoever she was. But no, she supposed that would
never do—besides, from his lack of reaction this
might be an everyday occurrence.

"Then you must be carried," said Harry triumphantly, and Almeria felt rooted to the spot.

A sudden cold draught of air made her realise
the fact that the door was being held open for her
by the servant, who seemed to be enjoying her discomfort. She turned to go, in a daze, as the foreign
lady's last words rang in her ears—"Help, help, I'm
ravished, ruined—!"

The heavy door closed with a thud behind her and she stood on the step a moment, unable to move. *Good gracious,* she thought, *poor girl!*—quite forgetting what her own purpose in calling upon Harry had been. A sharp gust of cold wind made her step slowly away from the house, sunk in the most alarming reflections.

Whatever her motives in calling that afternoon, and they had been of necessity vague, if hopeful, she had not really expected to be ravished there and then in the drawing-room—or wherever the two were—and so *publicly!* She had thought at least the door would be firmly shut on these occasions, if not actually locked. Small wonder ladies did not call unannounced on bachelors if that was what went on all the time! This unmistakable confirmation of Harry's rakish ways she did find rather appalling, she had to admit, however much she had been hoping to exploit these same tendencies herself. She had always cherished the notion, too, that gentlemen—even the most dissipated of gentlemen—exercised a certain discretion in their affairs by installing their mistresses in separate establishments. She had herself scarcely expected to move into Soho Square with Harry, not even in her most optimistic moments . . .

"Why, good afternoon," a familiar voice said, "it is Miss Denbury, is it not?"

She raised a startled wild-eyed face to Major Crispin Maunby.

10

Almeria felt quite convinced that if her heart had in truth been severely weakened by her recent disorder she must have fallen in a fatal swoon at Major Maunby's feet that afternoon. In a way, it would have been easier had she done so. As it was she had never been so confused in her life: aside from any other consideration she had supposed the major to be safely in Berkshire.

"G-good afternoon, sir," she managed to respond somehow. She hugged the fur muff to herself in the cold, and at the same time realised the 'note' she had been carrying was missing! This discovery

caused her to look over her shoulder in an alarmed
fashion, and she was only, she noted, about ten
yards away from the house entrance even now: the
major must have seen her descending the steps!

Crispin was almost as bereft of words as his companion; he simply could not imagine what had
brought Miss Denbury to call upon Harry on her
own. Then he remembered she had been unwell—
could that have any possible connexion with her
visit?—although he had no notion how. "May I
escort you anywhere, ma'am? You were not proposing to walk home alone, I trust?"

At least she could answer *that* question. "Oh no,
my carriage is waiting." She looked wildly about the
Square. "There! at the corner. I am on my way to
visit my sister Cordelia."

Upon hearing this Crispin turned about in order
to walk with her to the carriage. There was nothing
Almeria could do to prevent him.

"You are quite recovered from your recent indisposition, I hope?" He looked at her rather anxiously,
still baffled.

"Oh yes, thank you," she answered, so relieved
that he was evidently not going to refer to the extraordinary circumstance of her presence there. "Oh,
and I must thank you, also, for your thoughtful gift,
sir, it was most kind." She was astonished at her
ability to remember that, at the moment.

Crispin looked even more puzzled for a while,
as it was some little time ago that he had delivered

the melon to Bedford Square. "Oh, yes," he recalled with a smile, "that was really a joint offering from Sir Henry and myself."

If the Denbury carriage had not been coming towards them at some speed as he said this, Almeria would have been alarmed at the appearance of Harry in their conversation: she did not care to discuss him just now.

A very worried Bill-coachman drew up beside them with a flourish, as if he suspected Crispin of abducting his mistress. The groom jumped down, and recognising the major from his visits to Bedford Square greeted him with evident relief. He opened the door, and Crispin handed Almeria into the carriage.

"Good day to you, ma'am." He stood back and watched the carriage draw away, then made all haste to Harry to see what the old varmint had been up to, this time!

He took the steps to the front door two at a time. Tobin was in the hall, and as Crispin was removing his gloves he saw the servant looking in a perplexed manner at a piece of paper held in his hand: but he quickly bestowed it about his person and went towards the major to greet him.

"Sir Henry at home, is he, Tobin?"

"In the drawing room," was the reply, as the man took the hat and gloves, "but I don't think I would disturb him at the moment, sir he's—ah—having a somewhat diverting afternoon."

Crispin, having suspected that, waited eagerly for further enlightenment, but Tobin seemed to think he had already overshot the mark and he assumed his usual look of bland discretion.

"Yes, well tell Sir Henry I would like to see him later, if—"

"Cris—is that you?" Harry called from the drawing-room, where the door was still ajar.

With a quick involuntary glance at the servant, Crispin answered and went towards the drawing-room.

"Come in, come in," Harry commanded, cheerfully.

He went in, and was greeted by a scene of the most amazing domesticity. It was an overcast day and the room was illuminated by the glow from a huge fire: Harry was seated on one side of the ornate marble fireplace with a book in his hand, and on the other side was a prim-looking lady, also with a book, but her copy was open and she was peering somewhat short-sightedly at it in the dim light. Crispin saw she was clad in outdoor clothes; an expensive-looking silk pelisse and bonnet in the demurest lavender shade. What could be so diverting, he wondered, remembering Tobin's mischievous remark: it looked for all the world as if Harry was interviewing a governess!

The lady looked up uncertainly as the newcomer approached.

"Rosa, I think you've met Major Maunby, haven't you?" Harry put in quickly.

Crispin looked almost as uncertain as the girl when he realised who she was. Harry put aside the book and went to the bell-pull. "Miss Bezzolini has been helping me out," he told Crispin. "I think I am almost word-perfect now, and not before time, I may say!"

His friend's brow cleared: at least something was made plain at last. "Oh, I see, you've been rehearsing your part," he said, with a shade too much relief in his voice.

Harry favoured him with an ineffable look, but said blandly, "I have just been telling Rosa she can always turn actress now, if dancing begins to pall— she's astonishingly good." Tobin appeared at the door. "Ah, have a hackney summoned, would you? The young lady is leaving." He addressed Rosa as she turned to go. "I am not displeased with you this time, but it will be better if you do not call at the house again. Send me a note in the future, do you understand?"

She nodded vigorously, causing a momentary turbulence in the lavender ostrich feather curled about her bonnet. "Si, si, yes, signor, grazie." She gave Harry a dazzling smile, then dropped a hasty but impeccable curtsey to them both and tripped lightly from the room.

Crispin closed the door after her, and gave Harry

a speaking look as he went towards the welcoming
fire.

"Well, there's no call to view me as Flutter did
when you had been out all night, is there, you old
Mawworm? Help yourself to some cognac, for pity's
sake, and banish the pinched look!"

Crispin did so with alacrity, and poured another
for his friend; he felt they were both going to need
it. Rosa must have been there when Miss Denbury
called, but Harry looked remarkably unruffled by
the encounter. Added to which, he thought, Harry
was supposedly intent upon reforming his ways!
Precious little sign of it!

"Dammit, Cris, you look as though you've swal-
lowed a twopenny coachwheel!" Harry told him as
he took the glass. "I know it wasn't the thing to
have Rosa here, but what could I do? The dear girl
returned a valuable snuff-box which I'd left in her
apartment weeks ago. To tell the truth I was worried about it, as I hadn't the least notion where I'd
lost it. Well, understandably, she didn't care to
entrust the box to anyone else so she thought she
must bring it herself. When she arrived I was getting
into a rare pucker over my part as Loveless—the
first performance is tomorrow night at the Argyle
Rooms, as you know—and it seemed a heaven-sent
opportunity to have an impromptu rehearsal of
some of the scenes at least. There was no other lady
I could have approached for such help, I may say,
for it is a warm play in parts! Besides, it was by

way of being a final English lesson for Rosa—not that she needs much more tuition now . . . Anyway, what am I doing justifying my perfectly innocent actions under my own roof! Even you must own she looks the perfect pink of gentility."

Crispin thought that was scarcely the point: two genteel-looking ladies calling upon Harry in the afternoon would set the tongues wagging more surely than a bevy of Haymarket ware! But he merely agreed, and added, "Remarkable influence you have there." He took a gulp at the brandy.

"Did have," amended Harry. "I told you, I'm a reformed character now."

"Yes, I thought you were."

Harry looked at him through narrowed eyes. "And what is that spinsterish tone supposed to mean, pray? Ah, I know what it is—you're cantankersome because you leave for Berkshire and the bosom of your family in the morning."

"That has nothing to say to anything," retorted Crispin.

"No? But there is something! Come, Cris," Harry said coaxingly. "You can tell me, whatever it is— but I own I thought you had revised your habits as well lately. You haven't been playing deep again, have you?" Or was it, he wondered, mere flinching against committing himself finally to the married state?

"Now who's being spinsterish?" snapped Crispin, then he took the plunge before matters ran completely out of hand. "Harry," he said, with such a change of tone that his friend looked rather alarmed, "were there any other callers, this afternoon?"

Harry drew his brows together and looked at him intently. "No . . . why? were you expecting someone? You're not waiting upon being called out, are you? I'll be your second, you know that—"

In spite of himself, Crispin laughed. "Harry, what a lurid imagination you have got!" he cried, conveniently forgetting his own, which had been working rather hard that afternoon. "No, you are glaringly abroad in your conjectures; it is merely that when I came in just now I saw another young lady, leaving by the front door."

Harry stared. "Leaving *this* house, you mean? A young lady?" he repeated stupidly. When Crispin nodded, he jumped up and tugged the bell-pull violently. "We'll soon get to the root of this. Tobin has said nothing; what is he playing at, I wonder. Did you recognise this 'young lady'?" he asked suddenly.

Crispin looked even more uncomfortable. "I did, yes, but I'd rather not divulge her name, Harry, until I know more about the business."

"Well, we'll soon settle it, here's Tobin . . . Tobin, close the door—what's that you have there?"

"It appears to be a letter, sir, although I'm not at all sure where it came from. I found it on the floor in the hall by the fireplace."

"Let me see it—ah, it is directed to me." Harry tore it open, and Crispin waited for all to be made plain: it was deuced odd that Miss Denbury should be acting messenger-girl but at least it made some sort of sense. "Dammit, it's blank! What sort of cantrip is this, Tobin, answer me that?"

"I'm sure I don't know, sir."

"And Major Maunby tells me a young lady called here this afternoon," Harry said, trying to keep calm in face of mounting provocation.

"Yes sir, that's quite right. Lost a dog, she said, in our area."

"Dog? Oh," said Harry, considering this. "But we haven't got an area!"

"No sir. I'd beg leave to doubt that the young person had a dog, neither."

She has, thought Crispin, but he didn't judge it wise to intervene at the moment.

"Tobin," began Harry, in the controlled manner of one being driven to extremities, "I'm a reasonable man and not easily ruffled, but I wish you will tell me what the devil you are talking about!" he concluded in a shattering theatrical crescendo, much enhanced by his earlier rehearsing. He crushed the note and threw it from him.

"Yes sir." Tobin's thin face looked properly sober but Crispin noticed there was a certain gleam in his pale eyes. "The young lady rang the bell, and when I answered she asked to see you, sir. Upon being asked her name, she hesitated, then came out with the hoaxing tale about the lost dog. Well, I guessed it was all a hum, sir," he went on, watching his heavily-breathing master in a careful manner, "but thought the best way was to humour her, and save embarrassment. Not that it did that, in the event," he interposed, with a brief chuckle. "She looked a respectable-enough person, mind, quite well-bred, I would hazard. Well, I made as if to go below stairs but thought it was best to keep an eye on her, which I did. But she made no move to steal any-thing, indeed she didn't stir from the spot, so I told her there was no dog on the premises and she left," he finished a trifle lamely.

"It makes not a shadow of sense to me, but what makes you so sure it was all a hum, as you put it?" asked Harry, glancing from Crispin to his servant in exasperation.

"Well, it's my belief the young lady *did* want to see you—after all she asked for you by name—but when she heard you was engaged (and that wasn't difficult, sir, this door being open as it was) she said the first thing that come into her head. She was sufficiently up to snuff to know she shouldn't be here, of that I am certain." Tobin again had the look of one enjoying a huge joke. "In any event, I had the feeling she wasn't sorry to escape, sir," he couldn't resist adding.

An expression of dawning realisation had passed over Harry's dark face during this speech. "Tobin," he said heavily, "would you care to run your eye over these pages and tell me at exactly what point you left the young lady eavesdropping in the hall?" He handed him his copy of Vanburgh's *The Relapse*.

Harry exchanged a somewhat desperate look with Crispin over the servant's bowed head.

"There, sir," Tobin said, pointing gleefully.

"I thought so . . . and no doubt you were well aware—having heard it several times before—of the nature of that scene, and couldn't resist the opportunity it offered, you wicked old devil! You might at least have closed the door. Why, I could turn you off for less! Tobin," he went on with some sternness now, "did you know the lady? Have you ever seen her before?"

"No, sir," he answered, all amusement gone now as he saw his master's rare, steely look.

"You'll not breathe a word of this to anyone, understand. You were alone in the hall, I take it?"

"Yes sir."

"You may go." Harry watched his retreating back and as soon as the door shut, he swung round to face Crispin. "You'd best tell me who it was," he said resignedly.

"Dammit, Harry, I can't, you must see that! I should never have mentioned it, but how was I to know . . . Anyway," he said, his curiosity getting the better of him, "what *was* the scene you were rehearsing?"

Harry gave him the open book, then sat down

dejectedly: he picked up the crumpled piece of paper from the floor and stared at it, but it still told him nothing.

Crispin gave a shout of laughter. "No wonder you're blue-devilled—not a shred of reputation left after this afternoon's work, have you?" His shoulders still shook. "But for all that I can see why Tobin couldn't resist the temptation . . . Oh, Lord," he said suddenly, in appalled tones as he remembered who it was he had seen outside. "Why did she come here, I wonder?" he murmured.

"It's no use asking me *that,* is it?" said Harry quite savagely, "when I don't even know who it was. In fact, I don't know the first thing about any of it!"

Crispin struggled with his conscience: if he had not been leaving for Berkshire early next morning he might have been able to glean something to throw light on the affair from Mrs Wren, although it was a devilish ticklish matter to raise with any lady. On the other hand he was worried about the girl: could her illness have disordered her senses? He had gathered it had been of a pretty severe nature. But the family carriage had been there, of course, and she hadn't seemed unhinged—a trifle distraught perhaps, but that was understandable . . .

"Crispin, who was it? If this tale circulates in the town, I'm ruined! I might as well move to Scantleby Hall and take on Parfitt's mantle tomorrow!"

"Oh, it won't! I'm perfectly certain of that," Crispin said, but could he be sure? If the errand had been a legitimate one, would the girl go straight to her mother with tales of assault and rape in the Chirton establishment?

"Well, I'm not, and it is imperative I see this young lady and—Oh, I don't know!" He sighed and ran a hand through his dark hair. "Crispin, I'm waiting," he said quietly.

His friend sat down, took a deep breath and murmured, "It was Miss Denbury . . . Almeria Denbury."

Harry looked as though he didn't know whether to laugh or cry. "I don't believe it! Not the—" He cleared his throat and tried again, "not the fair young daughter, who is promised to the *clergyman?*" He emphasised the last word as if his ill-luck knew no bounds.

"Yes—no, that is, she is no longer betrothed, I collect."

"Well, that is some small consolation, I'm sure! The shy young Denbury, eh? But why? What brought her here?" he said, with an air of complete stupefaction.

11

It was fortunate for Almeria that Cordelia, never one to take a vast amount of interest in her young sister, was now wholly occupied with her own affairs. Almost as soon as Merry had arrived at Golden Square she was whisked up to inspect the waiting nursery. Between the: 'What do you think of this, Merry?' and: 'Is this not the prettiest cradle imaginable?' Almeria had no cause to worry that her sister might notice her distracted manner: an occasional murmur of admiration and word of agreement was all that was necessary.

Over refreshment, for which Merry was offered

wine ('to strengthen your poor nerves,' said Cordelia) and ratafia cakes, and the hostess self-indulgently consumed a quantity of Mrs Manners' brawn and a glass of goat's milk, the conversation quite naturally and undemandingly turned to Hec and the pups.

Until Almeria was settled in the carriage once more, homeward bound, she had had little time to ponder over her extraordinary visit to Soho Square. Luckily, it had been of very short duration, and that, coupled with the fact that Major Maunby had escorted her back to the carriage, she trusted would quell any curiosity Bill-coachman and the groom might have had about the call. In any event, she thought it best not to draw attention to the matter again and hoped they would not mention it to anyone.

But if the visit could be kept from her family's ears it seemed in the highest degree unlikely it would escape Harry's notice. If only she had not had the ill-fortune to encounter the major at that moment all might have been well—in some respects, at any event. Of Harry's behaviour she did not know what to think, but told herself sternly that with her own *laissez-faire* attitude she should not set herself to judge the conduct of others. After all, he had a perfect right to behave in any manner he pleased in his own home but *she* had had no right whatever to be there eavesdropping upon him. It brought a blush to her cheek every time she thought of those few minutes.

However, it was clear that for the moment there was nothing further she could do, except to hope the escapade was not brought to the notice of her family. As the evening progressed undisturbed she dared to think that at least the coachman and groom had kept silent on the matter, and as she had also discovered from Fanny that Major Maunby was definitely due to leave for the country the next morning—and they would not therefore be seeing him for some time—she went to bed a little less apprehensive than she had imagined.

By the morning, she had convinced herself the episode would be forgotten in a few days, but what she would do then was not at all clear to her. It was not that her feeling for Harry had undergone any change due to her discovery the day before, but she found it shaming enough to have to hurl herself at his feet without also being made so vividly aware she was one of a throng of ladies at his command. She had some pride left, she hoped, in spite of her tragically altered circumstances . . .

These thoughts were flitting through her mind when she was settled quietly in the morning-room, with her mama and Fanny, embroidering a counterpane for the cradle she had seen only for the first time the afternoon before. Encouraged by being able to imagine now the forget-me-not and rose design coverlet in Cordelia's pretty nursery she continued her work with renewed enthusiasm.

Hec and her little family had been removed from the morning-room closet, at Mrs Denbury's in-

sistence: their disruptive presence made it quite
impossible to receive visitors there with any peace
of mind, and they were banished to a lobby at the
back of the house. Almeria still had charge of them,
though, and had that moment returned from at-
tending to their wants: she was to wish she had
lingered over the task a little longer.

All three ladies were plying their needles in order
that Cordelia's first-born should want for nothing,
and when a carriage drew up outside in the quiet
square three heads were raised in unison.

"Now who is this calling, I wonder?" said Mrs
Denbury, mechanically. No one was expected and
Morgan's arrival was awaited without impatience:
it would be one of their many female acquaintances
come to gossip the morning away.

"It is Sir Henry Chirton to see you, ma'am,"
Morgan informed her in due course.

"Sir Henry? Well, what a pleasant surprise! Show
him in, Morgan."

Almeria pricked her finger, sucked it in a frantic,
unladylike fashion and fixed her eyes upon the doorway. He must have come to see what she had been
doing at his house yesterday. What could she say?
One of her mama's more sophisticated sayings—to
her own contemporaries—was 'the Lord loveth a
cheerful liar' but it was not to be supposed she
would encourage any of her daughters to put it into
practise on this or any other occasion: in any event,
thought Merry desperately, the main problem was to
invent any convincing story—cheerful or otherwise.

Certainly, none had sprung to mind by the time Harry was making his bow to her mama.

From the moment he had entered the room, though, he had sought her out and their gaze met in a seemingly conspiratorial fashion: Merry sensed it at once. Harry was not his usual assured and easy-mannered self; he refused the offer of a chair and, limping more noticeably than usual, went over to the window. He stood, a hand on the back of a chair, fingers tapping and with every sign of agitation, but always his dark eyes rested on Almeria. She found herself smiling at him: a smile which sprang partly from nerves, partly from a sudden feeling of sympathy and understanding for the uncomfortable position she had placed him in, but mostly because she couldn't help herself—she was glad to see him, whatever his purpose in calling.

Mrs Denbury began to wonder when they were going to discover precisely what their visitor had come for. After an exchange of commonplaces about the weather, Sir Henry enquired in tones of great concern of Almeria's state of health. The question was addressed to Merry but her mother was used to answering for her silent young daughter.

"Much improved, thank you, Sir Henry, she is able to go about once again and is as stout as ever she was, aren't you, my dear? Why, only yesterday afternoon she called upon her sister Cordelia and had a wonderful cose with her, I collect."

Fanny, noting her cousin's usual acute embarrassment at being singled out in this fashion, thought it incumbent on her to divert attention. "Has Major Maunby set out for Berkshire as he intended, Sir Henry?"

Harry focused his eyes on the speaker as if drawn back from a great distance. "Er—yes, before first light—luckily it appears to continue dry for his long ride." As he said these trite words he began to feel tolerably certain, looking at his hostess's untroubled expression and calm reception of him, that no word of her daughter's call had reached her at least: he would surely have been frowned upon if the merest whisper of Almeria's admittance to his house had come to her notice and, had the whole been communicated, he would of a certainty been denied entry to *this* house today and for the foreseeable future . . . As for Almeria herself, she appeared a trifle discomfited, it was true, but had she fled from his presence in disgust he would scarcely have blamed her: instead, she had favoured him with a smile of, it seemed, genuine warmth. He was in his turn discomfited by this. What was he to make of her behaviour? She had, on the face of it, cast her reputation to the winds merely to gain entrance to his house, and for what purpose he still could not imagine.

After a general and protracted discussion upon how long it should take Crispin to arrive at the family seat, Harry decided to disclose his purpose in calling as the omens, so far, seemed propitious.

"Mrs Denbury, ma'am, you have favoured me with several kind invitations in the past, and I

should like now to return the compliment if I may.
The notice is short, I fear, but I should deem it a
great honour if you and your family would accept
an invitation to attend an amateur performance of a
play at the Argyle Rooms tonight."

"But how delightful," replied Mrs Denbury, relieved that the purpose of his visit was made plain
at last. The apparent perturbation of the usually
urbane Sir Henry had been rather disquieting but
the cause was soon to be revealed. "As to its being
short notice, well I can hardly protest at that, can
I, for I gave you no more on one occasion!"

"I know you were rendered averse to play-going
by your unfortunate experience at Covent Garden,
but I can assure you this is a purely private affair
and in no way comparable." Harry smiled suddenly,
and Almeria had the gratification of again seeing
his eyes crease in the manner she found so endearing. "No, not in *any* way comparable in fact, as I
am to play the leading role!"

This announcement caused a great stir amongst
his audience, not least in Almeria who could
scarcely believe her good fortune: Major Maunby
could not have mentioned seeing her, after all.

"We shall be privileged indeed, Sir Henry, how
very kind of you to think of asking us. I'm sure we
shall be delighted to accept—except for Almeria,
of course, and I am not at all sure—" but here she
was interrupted, not by one, but two protesting
voices.

"Oh, mama, no, I *must* see Sir Henry!" Merry

cried, whilst Harry said in tones hardly less impassioned, "I had particularly hoped Miss Almeria could attend," then realising how this must sound to her startled-looking parent, added hastily, "for she is the great drama-lover of the family, I collect?"

"Well yes, she is," admitted Mrs Denbury. "Very well, I daresay it will do no harm." She glanced at her daughter, and in doing so intercepted the look which passed between the girl and Sir Henry: why, she thought, they have a decided look of complicity about them. Then, instantly, she knew: Almeria was in love with Sir Henry, there was no mistaking her rapt expression—and judging by his recent distracted behaviour, he with her! But how had it come to pass—? they had scarcely met above twice . . .

She was right about Merry, of course, but Harry's distraught manner had quite another cause: it was imperative Almeria should see him in *The Relapse* so that she should know it was merely play-acting she had overheard. This much, at least, had been decided during his long talk with Crispin on the matter, the day before. But, beyond the retrieval of his own battered reputation, he had not thought, although he was surprised at the shy young Denbury's apparently cheerful acceptance of his ramshackle behaviour: it was possible, of course, that she *did* know the piece already—according to Crispin she had an avid interest in the stage. "The play is one of Sir John Vanburgh's—*The Relapse*,

I daresay you may know it. My part is that of Love-less."

Mrs Denbury said, no, she did not believe she had ever seen it, Frances also shook her head, and Almeria announced she had not witnessed a Van-burgh play before but had read about the famous comedies, and was all impatience to see Sir Henry, particularly if he was going to appear in a periwig like Charles II.

This surprisingly long, not to say saucy speech from her daughter confirmed Mrs Denbury in her suspicions and further disconcerted Harry, who was beginning to revise his opinion about young Miss Denbury.

Having accomplished the prime aim of his call he bestowed tickets for the night's performance at the Argyle Rooms upon Mrs Denbury, and in addition invited the party to a private supper at the Claren-don after the play's completion. He was intrigued now by his young caller and wanted to get to the root of the matter if he could.

The Argyle Rooms were in Oxford Street and were not, in the ordinary way, a place for innocent young ladies: indeed there was a certain irony, Harry thought, in having to invite just such a young lady there to see a slightly indecorous play in order to absolve himself from the brand of libertine. Had Crispin been there for the performance—Harry's first in a leading role—they would both no doubt

have joined in the riotous party given at the Rooms
for the players afterwards. But his friend was absent
and he had decided to show a belated reverence for
the memory of the departed Hubert Parfitt in order
to cry off from the celebrations: instead he would
entertain the Denburys privately, and hope to discover more about Almeria. Until then, though, he
had enough apprehensions about his imminent
debut as Loveless to drive all other considerations
from his mind.

Mrs Denbury was not blind to the fact that the
Argyle Rooms were scarcely the place to take her
daughter, but she supposed Sir Henry must be ex-
cused this lapse in decorum as he was clearly
anxious Almeria should see his dramatic performance: but he must indeed be quite besotted, she
thought, to have risked a rebuff when he put forward the invitation that morning. That he had been
in expectation of some sort of disapprobation had
been obvious from his nervous demeanour. Mr
Denbury, however, was untroubled by the reputation of the Argyle Rooms and sceptical of his wife's
interpretation of Sir Henry's motives. "Depend upon
it, my dear, it is merely his way of compensating us
for a spoiled night at the theatre, and a dammed
thoughtful one, 'pon my word," he observed in his
benevolent way.

Frances accompanied the small family party, and
the four were treated with the utmost ceremony
upon their arrival at the Argyle Rooms that night.

They were shown to the best seats as befitted the particular friends of one of the leading players. There was no preliminary one-act play to endure as there would be at the professional theatres, and in no time at all the curtain went up on the small stage and the first scene of *The Relapse or Virtue in Danger.*

Merry had been in a wholly contented state all that day, for the first time since her illness and even long before that. She could not imagine why Harry had issued this invitation to them—or indeed, to *her* in particular, for there had seemed no doubt he had singled her out that morning. If only she had known, she could have waited just one more day and her indiscreet visit to Soho Square would not have been necessary. However, she forgot everything else as Harry made his entrance on the stage, and she prepared to wallow in the assured bliss of the next hour or two.

At first she found it difficult to believe it was Harry in that strange elaborate costume and periwig, although the voice was always unmistakable: she felt apprehensive, initially, that he would forget his lines but there seemed little danger of that as the play progressed. Mrs Denbury noted her daughter's total absorption with Sir Henry's performance and realised she need entertain no fears if the audience *did* respond occasionally in a ribald manner: she would not have been surprised if Almeria had not really heard one word of the play itself. This

judgement was abrogated, however, in the fourth
act when Loveless seduced Berinthia: she saw
Almeria's colour change rapidly and her hand lift
briefly to cover her burning cheek. It was scarcely
surprising the poor child was embarrassed, though:
she would not have thanked Mr Denbury had he
exposed *her* to such an unbecoming scene in their
courting days—her opinion of Sir Henry suffered a
slight decline.

Almeria's opinion of him, on the other hand,
positively soared as she realised what a hasty mis-
judgment she had made. Of *course* it was part of a
play she had heard, and why had she not noticed it
was a scene enacted at night with references to the
darkness—when it had been in the daytime she had
overheard it? Hard upon this realisation, though,
came the inevitable conclusion that *this* must be the
reason for her presence at the play, and that Harry
knew of her visit! She faced the supper a little less
blithely.

The Denburys were to precede Sir Henry to the
Clarendon in Bond Street and await his arrival
there. They were shown into a private room at this
superior and unexceptionable establishment—which
was in such marked contrast to the Argyle Rooms
that even Mrs Denbury was a trifle mollified: Sir
Henry had done his best to make amends, that was
as plain as pikestaff.

When he made his entrance some thirty minutes
later he was restored to the nineteenth century, al-

though still splendidly attired according to the mode of the day. Merry wondered that he had had time to achieve such an immaculately tied neckcloth, or to shrug himself into the glove-like blue tail-coat. His complexion, it was true, was somewhat heightened banishing his customary slightly sallow looks, but this was due to the hasty removal of the paint which had adorned it and, as he explained, he was very glad to have done with it.

Inevitably the talk was all of the play as they sat down to supper, and while Almeria half-listened she was reflecting that the lady who had appeared on the stage that night with Harry had no foreign accent, so that whoever had been with him at Soho Square must have been a *chère amie:* any sister, if he had one, would be English.

"—but I am interested to hear the opinion of the veteran devotee of the playhouse," Harry said, and Almeria realised he was looking at her in a quizzical manner.

With a colour she knew must match her dark red velvet gown (for no new resolution, however strong, could banish her blushes) she managed to reply: "I found it most enjoyable and very *instructive*. I cannot say how pleased I am to have had the privilege of seeing you act sir. I daresay you must have to do a vast amount of rehearsing beforehand to attain such a flawless performance." She was rather pleased with this impromptu speech: there was clearly no point in pretending to him she had not called at his house so she decided to brazen it out. She did not think he would refer outright—in present company—to the matter, and if he did she would have no alternative but to deny it, as there was still no plausible excuse she could put forward. She had in fact thrown herself on his mercy.

Harry could not but admire this retort, delivered with a degree of insouciance, although her pretty blushes belied her coolness. "Indeed I have," he responded carefully, "but I was fortunate in being able to call upon the assistance of the young Italian wife of one of my servants." That was a *quid pro quo* for Tobin, thought Harry with satisfaction, as he married him off in his imagination. "I have been teaching her English and it helped us both to read through the parts, as you imagine."

"But how kind in you, Sir Henry, to devote so much attention to your servants," commended Mrs Denbury. "I always believe the manner in which one treats one's people is most revealing of character." She went on to relate various instances known to her of indulgent masters and ungrateful servants, whilst the recipient of this encomium felt more and more thrown into the wrong over the whole ridiculous affair. He frowned over his wine-glass at the culprit but found himself contemplating such a crest-fallen face he revised his expression and smiled at Almeria: what an odd mixture the girl was, he thought. Even the dress she wore seemed at variance with her reputation—red velvet and silver lamé

would have been a probable choice of Rosa's, and
indeed would have suited her Latin looks a good
deal more than the fair honey blonde before him.

Merry, of course, had not wanted to wear that
particular gown, bought only to give Mr Tiffen a
disgust of her, but it had seemed the most suitable
for the Argyle Rooms. Since Harry's innocent explanation of the Italian girl's presence in his house
she had been relieved but also made to feel even
more guilty about her own conduct. The feeling of
mutual conspiracy was gone and she was left alone
in her transgression of decorous behaviour.

Robert Denbury cut across his wife's tales of
domestic trivia and commented on the excellence of
the fare at the Clarendon.

"Yes," said Harry, also glad to change the subject, "it is the only place where one may be confident of eating genuine French dishes. I find it
invaluable for returning hospitality. We bachelors
are at a grave disadvantage, you must know, when
it comes to entertaining at home."

Mrs Denbury thought, in the circumstances, this
might be a delicate hint that he was considering
marriage but she did not pursue it directly. "You
have a very fine house, I collect, in Soho Square?"

"Yes, ma'am, it is one of the earlier buildings—
seventeenth century, I believe, although the Chir-
tons have only had it since the beginning of the
last century. It is one of the houses *without* a base-
ment area to the front," he said with curious em-

phasis. "There are only one or two left now." Harry had not been able to resist teasing Almeria with this remark, and he glanced at her to see how she took it.

At the time she had not remembered to look for an area when she left the house—she had scarcely been in a state of mind to do so, and now this remark of Harry's removed any vestige of excuse she might have been able to offer. So, nothing loth now, she met his searching look with what she hoped was an enigmatic smile.

Certainly it baffled Harry, who was beginning to lose patience with the whole business. However, he was drawn back into the conversation again and found himself telling the company about his Scarborough house—but not about its late owner.

Mr Denbury knew the area, being a Yorkshireman—although not Mr Parfitt luckily—and Frances had some knowledge of Yorkshire so Harry was able to talk with her: a circumstance he had wanted to contrive as he was inevitably interested in Crispin's choice of bride. He could not but think her charming with a pleasing disposition but she lacked any great spirit and liveliness—not surprising in a young widow, of course, but he could not see her as a life companion of the ebullient Cris . . . Lord, he thought, it was a poor night's work at Covent Garden when he had so light-heartedly involved them both in the Denbury family's affairs.

12

Harry had two more performances to give as Loveless but when these were behind him, he found he was exhausted and quite unable to shake off the lethargy which threatened to sink him into a persistent depression of spirits. Tobin, still not entirely restored to favour, after being in Harry's black books for his sizable contribution towards his discomfiture with Almeria, had not seen him so hipped since he first came back from the war. Unfailingly, by this time of the year, the shutters would have been up and the knocker off the door, and Sir Henry—with Tobin—would be fixed at some country seat for a few weeks, for the pursuits of shooting and hunting, or billiards and dancing, depending on the weather, before moving on to another house and county. For Sir Henry was popular and there had never been any lack of invitations. Nor was there this year, as Tobin well knew, so why did he not accept them?

This was a question Harry was hard put to answer himself, as he slumped in his chair one morning, legs outstretched, and staring at the gleaming toes of his Hussar boots—for habit died hard and he was dressed to make his weekly call upon Tattershall's. He might just buy a prime hunter if one caught his eye at the sales: stocking the future stables of Scantleby Hall was his only occupation at the moment. It was a trifle easier than finding a wife, he reflected, putting out a hand to the pile of invitation cards and languidly looking through them yet again. *Dammit,* he thought, as he tried to hazard which country house party would most likely throw an eligible wife in his way, *this is no less a lottery than my scheme for Crispin was!* He did not want to dwell upon that subject, though, and was glad to see Tobin arrive with the day's newspapers.

The servant eyed the invitation cards optimistically, but no instructions for travelling were forthcoming and he left, no word having passed between them—an unusual and disturbing fact in itself, and Tobin shook his head sadly.

Harry took up the *Morning Post* and turned, at

last, to the announcements to see how others were faring in the matrimonial stakes. The name Margaret Venables took his attention at once and he checked apprehensively to see that Maunby didn't accompany it: surely *that* wasn't the reason Cris had gone home! No—it seemed the lady's choice had fallen elsewhere. Could that really have been because Crispin had declared now his intention of marrying another? Whatever the reason, he found everything was pointing to Cris offering for Mrs Wren on his return—if he had not done so already. A further indication was the disappearance of the dapple-grey horse from his stables and which, according to his groom, had been taken to the Denbury stables for Mrs Wren. Matters must be far advanced, indeed, if he was presenting the lady with a gift as valuable as a horse . . .

The upshot was that Harry did not go to Tatt's that morning but to Bedford Square. He told himself he was merely interested in promoting his acquaintance with Crispin's future bride but—if he would admit it—he had not wholly forgotten the young Denbury girl: there was something deuced odd there, he was sure of it.

Mrs Denbury was the only person to be unsurprised at Sir Henry's call: he had, she considered, let just the right interval lapse—a week was neither too ardent nor neglectful in an aspiring suitor.

On this occasion Merry was unaware of Harry's

arrival as she was engrossed with the pups trying
to make them lap up their milk whilst it was warm:
Hec was finding the demands of motherhood tiresome, and was fretting to be away from her family
—small though it was. Merry also wanted the pups
weaned so that she could take Hec for walks again
—possibly in the direction of Soho Square.

The first sign Almeria had of Harry's presence in
the house was the sound of his unmistakable voice
and her mother's, approaching the nether regions of
the house.

"Here's Sir Henry come to see us, my dear, and
with a particular wish to see the pups."

Had Almeria schemed for a week she could not
have contrived a more fetching scene for Harry's
eyes. The setting was a lobby, dismal enough in
itself, but enlivened with shelves supporting row
upon row of Mrs Manners' colourful preserves and
pickles, in serried ranks like an apothecary's bottles
and gallipots: in the midst of this homely cornucopia
was Almeria in her pink befrilled sarcenet gown,
crouched beside the black and white dogs, her
golden hair only loosely caught back from her face.
Harry, who had only seen her in formal and somewhat unflattering dress hitherto, was much struck
with the tableau and immediately put in mind of a
rustic picture by George Morland—a number of
which had been hung, incongruously enough, at
Scantleby Hall.

"They are an attractive sight, indeed," he com-

mented, ostensibly of the spaniels but his eyes still
on Almeria, who murmured a greeting.

"Sir Henry thought he might have a pup when I
told him of them," Mrs Denbury explained.

"Yes, for I'm sure it will be incumbent upon me
to have a pack of spaniels at my heels when I move
into Scantleby Hall—but someone else must have
the training of this one, for I am no countryman, I
fear."

Merry had been delighted he was interested in
the dogs for that would be a future link, but this
further announcement was a blow: she had heard
about his acquisition of the Yorkshire house, but
did not know he was to move there.

"Do you intend to quit town then, Sir Henry?"
she asked baldly, drawing a look of censure from
her parent.

"Maybe," he parried, "I'm undecided about my
plans for the winter as yet." He was equally inde-
cisive about which pup to have for they were both
dogs, and as he said—"They look alike as two peas
to me."

"But to me they are not," Merry told him. "You
shall have this one," she said, picking up one twin,
"for he has by far the most powerful intellect."

Harry smiled. "Well, I hope he does not outshine
me, that's all! I want no youthful prodigies," he
protested with sudden emphasis, his thoughts flying
off at a tangent to his nephew, Henry, the nursery
philosopher.

They then left the spaniels and returned to the morning-room, where Frances was quietly sewing.

Harry had been surprised that Mrs Wren had evinced no apparent interest in Crispin as yet, so he said: "I have had no word from Major Maunby since he left for Berkshire, but I daresay I shall hear when he is planning to return." Crispin had teased Harry by not divulging this information before he left, and he thought Mrs Wren might have the advantage of him there: but she hadn't, it seemed, or at least was not prepared to admit it.

"I think he was a trifle uncertain about the duration of his visit," Fanny said, smoothing a stray blonde hair from her forehead. "It depended, I collect, on the reception he was given."

Harry thought it diplomatic not to pursue that line. "Yes, well, in his absence I thought you might care to come out—with your cousin" (he looked briefly at Almeria)"—for a drive through the parks occasionally. The weather can be inclement at this season, I know," he acknowledged hastily to Mrs Denbury, "but an hour or so round the parks when it is fine could do no harm, I'm sure."

"Oh yes, that would be lovely, wouldn't it, Fanny?" Almeria cried, a look of pure delight on her face, which startled Harry until she added: "It is just what Hec needs—I may take her for a run in the park when we get there, may I?"

"Surely," he agreed readily.

Fanny, to whom the invitation had been issued

primarily thanked him, but she, as well as Mrs Denbury, now was beginning to think Sir Henry and Almeria were showing a marked interest in each other.

That this was so on Merry's side was to be proved beyond doubt on their first drive out with him. The arrangement had been that Harry should call at eleven on the first day which promised to be dry and clear.

Never had Almeria taken such a passionate interest in the climate: it was after all almost the end of November and perhaps there would be *no* fine days before Christmas! Since her illness she had lived from day to day, savouring every moment she could, and with no thought to any future; but now there was an added urgency if Harry was liable to quit London soon, so it was not surprising she was all impatience for a break in the overcast wet weather. In the event it was only four days coming but it seemed like a lifetime to her.

Harry, on the other hand, had been vastly relieved that he had been granted a few days' grace before taking the Denbury ladies for a drive. The offer had been impulsively made: indeed, he was not wholly sure now, why he had been so rash. His barouche—a more sedate vehicle than the racy curricle he usually employed for himself and one passenger—had not been used for some years and needed renovation before it was in a fit condition to take to the road again.

However, all was ready in time and, as he drove his usual pair of raven black horses towards Bedford Square, he was not sorry he had made the effort. He did not want to appear to be poaching on Crispin's preserves as far as Mrs Wren was concerned, but he did still want to try and discover a little more about her, and a drive in the barouche together with her young cousin was surely the most unexceptionable way to achieve this: they could converse as Miss Denbury walked the dog in the park.

Later, as they bowled along in the crisp autumn air he wondered why he had had to justify the outing: what could be more enjoyable than driving in Hyde Park with two remarkably attractive ladies —particularly as the alternative was a day spent wondering yet again what his future plans should be.

Merry, who was no longer troubled by future plans, was as happy as she ever expected to be. She chatted animatedly with Fanny about the passing scene, but her eyes were usually fixed on Harry's back and the many-caped box-coat he wore. They had just passed Apsley House, a large red brick mansion on the periphery of the park, and were waiting briefly at the lodge at the Hyde Park Gate entrance.

"At least it is not the press of carriages and riders we would meet with on Sunday, although it is busy enough," Fanny commented, as they edged towards the lodge.

"I have never liked the Promenade, when everyone is out merely in order to stare at everyone else —and the gentlemen ogle the ladies in the most shocking fashion imaginable," declared Merry, recalling some embarrassing drives made in the family carriage in the early summer.

This was as nothing to the embarrassment she suffered at that moment, though. Harry had been exchanging good-natured badinage with the lodge-keeper, to whom he was apparently very well-known. The ladies had not been listening but it was impossible not to hear the parting shot, as they drew level with the keeper and he cackled impertinently: "—not called Old Harry for nothing, eh, sir?"

Almeria was ready to sink, and could not avoid a quick glance at her companion to see if she had heard, and if so, if it had meant anything to her: she had, and it did . . .

"Well!" Fanny murmured in a stupefied way, as she tried to piece together the sequence of events which had led them to be in Old Harry's barouche from that first admission of Merry's—months ago— that she had a hopeless tendre for a gentleman bearing that name. That it was no longer so hopeless seemed undeniable, and from being two ladies out for a morning drive they had been transformed into a young lady and chaperon, and Fanny misliked her role. All this had flashed through her

mind in a few seconds and Merry was saying urgently: "Forget what I told you all that time ago, please!—and don't breathe a word to anyone, will you?"

Fanny tried to see her cousin's face as she said this, but the deep poke of her bonnet was an effective shield, and at that moment the barouche halted again.

Harry turned on the box. "Here we are ladies! Shall we walk now?"

It was a rhetorical question and Merry's hand was on the door catch before the groom could step down to open it.

Hec bounded out at once, not the least excited member of the party as it was her first outing in weeks. Harry put the horses in the charge of his groom and said they would be back within the half-hour; then diplomatically placed himself between the two ladies so as not to favour one or the other.

They set off toward the Serpentine. At first the conversation did not prosper: Fanny was still preoccupied with her new-found discovery about her companions: Almeria, although anxious to talk to Harry, had been momentarily distracted also by the unwelcome revelation, and consequently Harry found his random remarks did not flourish.

But Hec soon altered that by suddenly taking exception to a cow grazing some distance away. It was a half-hearted charge, though, and she was clearly relieved when Harry caught up with her and carried her back to Almeria.

"You'd best leash her," he said, somewhat breathlessly as he had been encumbered by his great driving-coat: he was sorely tempted to add something about getting lost in area basements, but didn't.

"I'm so sorry—she doesn't usually behave like this—although I haven't had her for very long," Merry admitted. "I hope your leg came to no harm —does it pain you?"

"Hardly ever," Harry said shortly. "Tell me about this doughty beast of yours," he commanded.

Almeria laughed at this, for nothing could look more inoffensive than the spaniel tripping along at her heels. She told Harry about how she came to possess the dog, and in doing so revealed a great deal about herself and her family. She quite forgot her cousin's presence on Harry's other hand, and found herself talking to him like an old friend— which indeed he was to her. She found he listened attentively to what she said, too, a novelty to one who was accustomed to being ignored.

Fanny, who knew of Almeria's habitual taciturnity with strangers, was amazed at this flow of conversation and began to be still more suspicious: had she been meeting him clandestinely? But no, that must be out of the question—Merry never went out alone and anyway had been confined to the house for months. Besides, he clearly had not known

much about her before this walk—although that
omission had been fully remedied by the time they
returned to the carriage!

There was a slight air of constraint between the
two ladies on the return journey. Harry, up on the
box, was unaware of this, of course, and as he set
them down at the door of their house he asked if
they would like to repeat the excursion the next
fine day.

Merry immediately accepted with enough enthusiasm for both; but Fanny thanked him and said
in a quiet voice she would like that very much.

When they were indoors shedding their muffs,
bonnets and warm pelisses in the morning-room,
Almeria said impulsively: "Thank you, Fanny, I
thought you might refuse, and I don't think I could
have borne that!"

She eyed her young cousin thoughtfully. "That's
as may be, but I'm not at all sure I did the right
thing. I am quite in the dark over your attachment
to Sir Henry and do not know what sort of havey-
cavey business has been afoot."

"None!" cried Merry, but not entirely without a
feeling of guilt. "Besides," she said, going on to the
offensive, "*you* were able to ride with Major Maunby
and cast out lures to him—oh, I know you will say
'that is quite different', but you haven't announced
your betrothal to him yet although it is obvious—"

Fanny was looking at Almeria in a stunned
fashion. "Merry!" she said sharply, "curb your

tongue, do! You have been leaping to conclusions
on the scantiest of evidence! I did *not* cast out lures
to Major Maunby, nor have I the least expectation
of being betrothed to him—in fact I have no plans
to see him again, even."

Merry's amber eyes were rounded in consternation. "I'm so sorry, Fanny, I honestly did think
when you were in each other's company so much,
and . . . and there's the horse!—was not that a
gift from the major?"

"No it was not," Fanny declared in exasperation.
"I paid for that from my own pocket." She went
over to the fireplace and spread her hands before
the flames. "The major is an excellent judge of
horseflesh and could not have chosen a better mount
for me than the grey. I hired it at first but when—"
She checked momentarily, then went on, "I decided
to buy it when our rides came to an end. He offered to accompany me on short outings when you
were ill—I think because he was sorry for me,
really, and there was a kind of bond between us
from his acquaintanceship with my late husband,
you know. However, I am perfectly certain there
was no thought of any attachment in either of our
minds . . . Anyway, to return to the matter of my
mount. I wanted a saddle-horse and I knew Uncle
Denbury would have been only too pleased to have
acquired one for me—but you know your papa!
Had I done that he would most likely never have
allowed me to pay for it—or even told me how

much it was. I am beholden to your family enough already, Merry, you do understand that, don't you? And," she concluded in a short burst of defiance, "I like to retain a little independence of my own."

Merry stood a little way behind her cousin and watched her rather sadly: she thought she had discovered some new happiness at last in meeting the major. "I truly am sorry, about everything—misunderstanding the situation and—well," she floundered, "I thought you had found someone again."

Fanny turned her head and with a smile of supreme contentment said softly: "But I have, Merry. Mr Tiffen and I are to be married."

13

Almeria was surprised into complete silence on hearing Fanny's news; and her cousin, feeling she might be affronted that Mr Tiffen should have consoled himself so readily after her rejection of him, explained: "We have not announced this sooner because of it coming so fast on the heels of Mr Tiffen's offer for you: I own it must look a trifle odd. Your parents know, of course, as a matter of courtesy, but we do not intend to publish our intention until the New Year. Jonathan is due to take up his Hampshire living then, and we shall marry and move into the parsonage right away."

This speech had given Merry chance to recover herself. "Fanny, I am so glad for you! You must know I should not mind, for I told you I was quite determined not to have Mr Tiffen."

"Yes," Fanny said, with eyes shining, "I shall always remember that moment—it was such a *relief*, I cannot express."

"When did you fall in love with him?"

"Oh, it's impossible to say . . . we always dealt well together, but he was forever at this house when you were unwell, you know, and I suppose it must have been then we became attached."

"Well," laughed Almeria, "I was blind to the last, as usual! But I do see now that it is an admirable match—I'm sure you'll be very happy."

There was a moment's pause, and both ladies drew a chair to the fireside and sat down.

"Before this confession was drawn—I might even say dragged!—from me, we were discussing you and Sir Henry, I collect," Fanny reminded her.

"*You* were trying to, certainly," Merry countered lightly, but her heart was heavy as the implications of her cousin's news became clear. She had expected a link of sorts to be forged between herself and Harry if Fanny had married his friend, the major, but now, not only was that opportunity lost, but she would be left on her own in the New Year with no companion—or chaperon—other than her mother. Her chances of seeing Harry might be slim indeed, and then only if he did not remove to Yorkshire. It was essential she make the most of these drives, although even as she thought this, another aspect of the situation occurred to her. Could *Harry* be attracted to Fanny? At the Clarendon supper she had noticed how he had engaged her in conversation rather more than was to be expected. And he had directed the invitation for the drives first and foremost to her cousin—'in the major's absence' he had said—but why, if he was not hoping to fix her interest himself? Well, it was an ill-wind, as her mama might say, and Merry intended to make full use of the future drives to captivate Harry—and with a clear conscience, too, as Fanny was promised elsewhere.

"Well, I cannot imagine how you have contrived it," Frances was saying, "but you appear to have a notable *parti* in Old Harry, as you called him. How *did* you accomplish it?"

"You are quite out in your reckoning, I have neither contrived nor accomplished *anything!*" But not for the want of trying, she thought bitterly. "Sir Henry is Old Harry, as you guessed, but he was quite chance-met at the theatre, as you know—you were there. I had seen him before at various plays, that is all. I am perfectly certain he is not taking us for these excursions for the pleasure of *my* company; he particularly asked you, in the first instance, did he not?"

"So he did, but I fancy that might have been his way of going about things—he had previously made

a most pointed invitation to you, remember, when
he asked us all to the Argyle Rooms. You cannot
deny that."

Merry could not deny it, but she could explain
it only too easily—and she still wondered if he
would broach the matter of her visit to his house,
when the opportunity arose . . .

"No, I cannot believe Sir Henry has the smallest
intention of making love to me," Merry declared
flatly. "So you may continue the drives without any
qualms—please," she added.

"Gladly! For when shall I again have the chance
to drive in such a splendid equipage when I am
established in my parsonage?" Fanny said this with
no trace of discontent, though, and was clearly very
happy with the prospect of being a parson's wife.

Harry presented himself, with the barouche, at
eleven-thirty sharp the next morning, and the trio—
with Hec—spent another enjoyable morning together, but this time he took them to St. James's
Park. They drove along the new road which had
only been laid the year before; and later, as they
walked by the canal to the old wooden Pagoda
bridge, Harry told them of the Grand Fête which
had been held there, for the road's opening, and
which the ladies had not attended. It was but a short
step in the discussion from fêtes to theatres, and in
no time at all Fanny found herself playing second
fiddle again, as her companions rattled on about the
merits and faults of players and performances. She

could not find it in her to begrudge Merry this pleasure, and willingly kept silent and admired the view . . .

The outing was over once more, and amazingly soon for Almeria, and although she had talked to her heart's content with Harry, she could scarcely pretend she was one jot further along the road to becoming his mistress! There was no doubt he regarded her as a well-bred miss and would never dream of making her any proposal other than marriage—which was out of the question. For if he should love her enough to contemplate making her his wife (and he would hardly propose to her for any other reason, as she was blessed with neither wealth, rank nor beauty) she knew she would not accept him. It would be too cruel—and quite improper to mislead him on her precarious state of health, even assuming her parents would contemplate marriage for her. It was no use, she had to accept that she was faced with an intractable problem which no amount of effrontery and brazen behaviour on her part would solve.

Her feeling of hopelessness was increased by the return of the inclement weather and no possible prospect of drives in the park while it continued. However, Mrs Denbury was holding one of her card-parties that week and Harry was included in the guests. That evening had been, Almeria thought afterwards, the happiest of her life, and one she would remember always. Her mama partnered her with Harry for whist, but for what reason Merry could not guess at. She thought it must be a desire on her part to produce an evenly matched game (for Harry was a dazzling player and she was not) mingled with pity for her, perhaps, as she no longer paid any attention to the fact that her feelings for Harry must be obvious to all. Mrs Denbury's kind and considerate attitude to Almeria still prevailed, and Merry took this as continuing proof of her fatal condition.

In the event, they had had a triumphant evening, winning all but two games. She cared nothing for what anyone thought of her and this had the salutary effect of banishing all nerves: she had, as Harry had put it, 'played like an angel'.

Well, she thought wryly, the last thing she wanted to be was an angel—of any sort.

The arrangement for their morning excursions still held good after the whist-party but the weather continued unco-operative: until one day, when the season had already advanced into December, brought a brilliant morning of hard blue sky and clear frosty air. The sort of day which banished the evil smells temporarily from the London streets and rendered them wholly delightful to Almeria.

There was, though, a hindrance in the way, and it arrived in the form of a note of invitation to Fanny from Mr Tiffen to join him and his uncle in the forenoon. It was not unexpected but Merry had feared it would fall on a fine driving day. The Tiffen uncle was a valetudinarian, and this had necessitated giving short notice for the visit so that he could be introduced to Fanny on one of his 'good days'.

"Pray don't send a message to Sir Henry cancelling the drive," Merry pleaded quite shamelessly to her mama, who exchanged glances with Frances.

"Well, it is not the thing for a young lady to be seen unescorted in an open barouche, you know, and Sir Henry would not like it," Mrs Denbury told her.

"But if I were to take Meg with me, I should not be unescorted, should I? Oh, please, mama!"

Mrs Denbury appeared to weigh the argument. "Very well, my dear—I would come with you myself but I still feel the cold abominably, as you know, after all those years in India."

Harry, although he showed no surprise, was a little taken aback to have Almeria put into his sole charge with only a young maid for chaperon, but if her mama raised no objection, he had no intention of doing so. He did show some surprise, however, when, as soon as they had turned into Great Russell-street, his groom called out to him to stop. Before he knew where he was Almeria had clambered up beside him on the box.

"I hope you do not object, sir, but Meg's conversation is a dead bore, and I had much rather talk to you."

"I am flattered, indeed," Harry chuckled sardonically, "but what of your reputation? If anyone should see us—"

"Oh, I do not regard that, believe me!" she told him fervently. "Please drive on, your horses will take a chill."

"Yes, ma'am, if you say so," Harry said in meek tones, and wondered when he would see a sign of this young lady's former diffidence.

"I wanted to have a private word with you and it is *so* difficult with all this punctilio one has to observe constantly," she confided in an airy way. "It is different for gentlemen, if they wish to pay court to a lady they are free to do so—"

"Within limits," Harry protested, "if they do not wish to compromise the lady in question." He felt a trifle unnerved.

"Yes, I suppose so, and that in turn must restrict them to the society of demi-reps if they do not wish to marry," she said in practical tones.

Harry glanced at his passenger, his dark brows raised in amazement, and was glad the road ahead was not busy. "Well, I can see why you did not care to be overheard! But what is this private word you are seeking?—If you think you are altogether wise to continue," he cautioned, not with a hint of amusement in his voice.

"Oh yes," Merry said blithely, "for that is quite unconnected. I was just riding my hobby-horse, you must forgive me." Before Harry had time to do so, she went on, "Can you be trusted with a secret?"

"I believe so, but are you quite sure . . .?"

"It might be important to you, I thought. You see Frances, Mrs Wren, is to marry a Mr Tiffen—you have met him, I believe." From the startled way he reacted she was sure that *was* the reason he had suggested these drives—to further his suit with Fanny.

Harry slowed the horses to an easy pace. "You are sure?"

"Perfectly. Oh dear, I shouldn't have announced it so heedlessly. I was right, wasn't I, it is important to you?" Merry asked, with an anxious frown: even on this subject she hated to cause him pain.

"Yes—well, no, not to me, precisely," Harry said, unusually flustered by this bizarre conversation. "I had the idea Mrs Wren's affections might be engaged elsewhere, that is all."

"Oh, so did I! Your friend, Major Maunby, you mean," she elaborated, as incautiously as ever.

"Look, I'm not at all sure we should be discussing our friends in this manner!"

"Frances won't mind, I'm sure, and besides you won't repeat it to anyone, will you?"

"Indeed, I will not! But might I ask why you thought it could be so important to me?"

"Well," she said, having the grace to hesitate momentarily this time, "I did wonder if perhaps you were dangling after Mrs. Wren yourself, you see," she burst out with alarming frankness, "for I could not imagine why else you should have invited her for these drives."

Harry favoured his companion with an ineffable look but was silent.

"I'm sorry, I shouldn't have said that, either! That's my trouble, I fear, I always say what's in my mind without a thought for the consequences. That's why I usually find it easier to stay silent," she confessed ruefully.

"Well, yes, if that is your habitual style I can see it would have its problems in polite society," Harry agreed, with a gleam in his eye. "But," he added swiftly, "since candour is the order of the day, perhaps you could tell me something."

From the tone of his voice Merry had a presentiment he was going to advert to the one subject she had hoped to avoid: but there, it was a risk she had taken with this forthright approach. She steeled herself, and murmured, "I will try."

"It is merely this—I wish you will explain why you called upon my house, and—even more inexplicable, if I am right—why you left a blank piece of paper behind directed to me? It was your note, was it not?"

"Yes," she admitted between her teeth.

"But why?"

"I—I wanted to talk to you," she said, throwing caution to the winds.

"I see," Harry said slowly.

"You don't."

"No—I don't . . . Look, I may be a member of the Four-in-Hand Club but I'm finding it increasingly difficult to attend to the horses. Do you mind if I drive quickly to the park—it is not far now—and then we can continue this interesting dialogue, and I can give it the undivided attention I feel it needs?" he concluded drily.

She shook her head. "No, please do." In theory, this gave her time to compose a plausible explanation, but she knew that was impossible—there *was* no plausible explanation. The noise of the carriage flying at speed over the stones luckily rendered any further comment difficult. Merry knew she faced the *dénouement* of her scheming and she hoped she would have the nerve to tell Harry the truth: but when the groom had handed her down from the box and she waited whilst Harry changed the driving gauntlets for York tan gloves, she thought she had never seen anyone of more outstanding propriety and elegance; she quailed at the prospect of making any improper disclosures to him.

Meg handed over Hec into her mistress's care and walked, as earlier instructed by Merry, at a good respectful distance behind the couple.

"I'm sorry," said Harry at once, "I really had no right to ask you point blank about your call. You were put to the blush at the time by my incompetent and ill-mannered servant—who, you will be glad to hear, had a thorough roasting for his pains —and I do not wish to cause you any more discomfort by referring to the matter again. I could not help but be puzzled by the affair, but my prime concern is for you—and your reputation, I may say, which can scarcely be enhanced by such visits."

"I do not regard that! I dislike intensely being hedged about with all this punctilio!" she said violently.

"Ah yes, your hobby-horse! But my dear girl," Harry felt bound to protest, "your good name will be in tatters. You will put to flight any honourable suitor—of which I am sure you have—Oh, lord," he muttered, remembering the changeable Mr Tiffen.

Merry guessed what he was thinking. "You need not torment yourself on *that* head," she said bitterly. "I had never the smallest desire to marry Mr Tiffen and did my utmost to repel him by my vulgar behaviour! But that had little effect, I fancy, until my ill-health made papa declare off on my behalf. I shall never marry now, so the problem of unsullied reputation does not arise. I intend to be as reprehensible in my ways as I wish."

Harry stared at the innocent-looking *enfant terrible* at his side in bewilderment: there was utter conviction in her voice and yet it did not make any sort of sense. Mr Tiffen had presumably transferred his affections somewhat mercurially, and her malady had been used to pluck her from the betrothal with propriety. "But you are so young—you must not jeopardize your whole future for the sake of a few youthful prejudices and the desire to shock every-one! You must think of the future—why, in two or three years I'd hazard you'll be wed to a gentleman of the first consideration, and be the very pink of gentility and moral rectitude." Harry was quite pleased with this bracing speech, and therefore was completely unprepared for his hearer to burst into a flood of tears.

Almeria buried her face in her muff and was absolutely furious with herself for suffering this recurrence of her weakness. How could she play the wanton minx with a red nose and swollen eyes? She couldn't: but then she had known she would not have the effrontery in any event. Her sobs redoubled, and Harry produced a handkerchief and said, "I'm sorry—let me call your maid."

Merry raised her head sufficiently to take the handkerchief and say, "No!" with great vigour and little gratitude. "I shall be all right in a m— moment." With a prodigious effort she regained her composure: there was nothing a gentleman disliked more than a weeping woman, she knew that.

"Shall we return to the barouche?" he asked. "I dare say you are not wholly recruited after your recent indisposition, which was of a severe nature, I collect." He felt to offer overt sympathy at this stage would be fatal.

"I'd rather walk, thank you." She looked at him, an almost pleading expression on her face. "Do you know what my ailment was?" she asked with genuine interest.

"Why no," he said, surprised. "How should I?"

"How should you, indeed, when *I* do not know myself." She sounded very weary.

"But I find that very strange—did you not ask?"

"No, for there was little point. I should not be told the truth."

"I cannot believe that," he began soothingly.

She did not want any soft words. "Will you, then, if I tell you I have only two years to live?" she snapped, and then added, "at the most," as a pathetic afterthought.

Harry was appalled. "But who can possibly say? Besides, if you don't know what ailed you—" She did look a little pale, and had always had a fragile aspect: perhaps it was true . . .

"The doctor said so, I heard him," she said tonelessly. "When I was drugged—they thought I was asleep, I expect." It was odd, talking about it. It was the first time she had shared her fears with anyone, and the last person she had wanted to know was Harry. Her lips quivered again.

Clearly something had to be done, thought Harry; she would fret herself into a decline even if her fears were baseless. "Pay no heed to quacks! If the fellow who tended my shattered leg had been right I had only a few months at my disposal at most—but here I am! A bit the worse for wear, it is true, but that does not signify. Threatened men live long, they say."

"Oh, pray stop! You sound like mama."

"I'm sorry—"

Poor Harry, she thought, I should never have told him. "No, forgive me—it was wrong of me to mention it. I do not know why I did for it cannot concern you."

This gave Harry an idea. "No, I think you have done quite the best thing in telling me for, as you say, I am not closely involved," he said in matter-of-fact tones. "If I were to find the truth of the matter would you believe *me* if I told you? I swear I should not sugar the pill—I should want to know the truth, however unpalatable, if I stood in your shoes."

Almeria had a painful constriction in her throat but she managed to say, "Yes . . . I would, thank you."

14

Almeria and Harry returned to the carriage immediately after he had made this promise to her, and the subject was not reverted to again. Merry made a determined effort to talk of other things, though, and Harry, admiring her pluck, responded to her lead. Nonetheless, she drove back with Meg, who was agape with silent curiosity, and left Harry to his thoughts on the driving box.

On her return home she felt quite prostrated; in fact so feeble and tearful as to be apprehensive she might be succumbing to her weakening affliction again. However, Mrs Denbury ascribed her perished look to the cold, and briskly revived her with some hot soup.

Merry had not thought much at the time as to how Harry was to discover the truth of her malady, but it was obvious he would have to apply to her mother: an idea she did not altogether relish, for why should Mrs Denbury discuss her daughter with Sir Henry? The more she thought about it the more it became clear he would be fobbed off with platitudes, as she would be herself.

Harry had said he would acquaint her with his tidings at the first opportunity, but that he deemed it advisable to discontinue their drives until the matter was settled; an arrangement she willingly complied with, as she had created a situation of intolerable awkwardness between them with her weak-minded confession.

But then, to her surprise, the next day her mother announced an impromptu card-party, to be held the following evening. Friday was the customary day for this event but on this occasion it was fixed for Wednesday. "It seems Sir Henry is engaged for Friday," Mrs Denbury explained, "and you know what an asset he is to any whist-party. It is well worth altering the day, you must agree, Almeria."

"Has he accepted at such short notice?" she asked, fairly certain he would not wish for an encounter any more than she did.

"Indeed, yes! It will be a small gathering, but none the worse for that."

By the time the evening of the party came, Merry was seriously contemplating falling back upon her old trick of having the headache, so that she need not face Harry: it would not be altogether untrue for she was full of apprehension as to what he might discover. She had complete faith in him to tell her the truth—should he be in possession of it— and this period of waiting was an ordeal.

She was sitting in front of her dressing-table mirror—too apathetic to change yet for the evening. Studying her features intently she wondered if they would tell her anything: after all, it was said death was written in people's faces sometimes—a churchyard skin—but perhaps only others could see it . . .

Meg came in. "Pardon, miss, but can you go down to the morning-room, please, mistress says?"

"But I'm not ready—"

"At once, miss, Mrs Denbury said, whatever you was doing."

"Very well, Meg. The guests haven't arrived yet, have they?"

But Meg was gone.

Merry swept into the morning-room, feeling a bit cross to be interrupted: she could not appear at the gathering, however small, in her pink sarcenet morning gown.

"Is it important, m—?" she began, then checked. Harry was alone in the room, an elbow on the mantel and looking in great good humour.

"I'm sorry," she began again, but Harry said, "Yes, it is important, ma'am."

"Oh, I see." This was the moment, then, when she was to be told: was his smile one of desperate reassurance or genuine relief? Her legs felt rather weak suddenly and she sat down, telling herself, as her old nurse would, *I must be brave* . . .

Noting her expression, Harry said quickly: "I shall not draw out your apprehensions for a moment longer—I have made all inquiries that are feasible into your expectation of life, and I can assure you you have no cause to fear any evil consequences from your recent disorder, and that," he went on, forestalling any objections, "is the considered verdict of your doctor and both your parents: and I cannot help but agree with them, having heard the whole unfortunate tale now."

But Merry, in spite of saying she would believe him implicitly, and meaning it, when it came to the point she found she could not do so. All she had achieved was to offer her family a splendid opportunity to reassure her through Harry's agency. What it amounted to was that she could believe bad news but not good. "How can you be so sure? Can you tell me precisely what you discovered?" She did not wish to show outright rejection of his word and thus offer him an insult.

But Harry was not deceived. "I thought you'd not believe me, you gudgeon!" he said with a rueful smile. "But yes, I can give you chapter and verse

. . . You were attended, as you know, by two doctors. The first, I collect, was summoned shortly after the onset of your prostration, and selected solely because that gentleman had, on an earlier occasion, successfully prescribed some eye snuff for your papa for an irritation of the eyes. The Denburys, I am given to understand, for the most part enjoy the rudest health," he interposed, "and so have no vast experience of the faculty. However, it soon became clear that for anything more comprehensive than an eye affliction this particular member of the faculty had one remedy only—and that was bleeding. Now, I don't pretend to know the efficacy of that treatment in all circumstances, but I am tolerably sure it is not the universal panacea this quack of yours deemed it. I have seen some disastrous results from the method . . . In the event, your parents judged him to be chiefly concerned with prolonging your low condition until he could prescribe daily phlebotomy for you—and burgeoning bills for himself. What more natural then, when told to cut his stick, he should take huff and forecast doom and disaster, in the most venomous fashion, after his departure. *That* pretty speech is no doubt the one you overheard—and what a tragedy it was!"

Almeria's gaze had been fixed on Harry's face throughout this explanation, and she found she had scarcely dared to breathe for most of the time. She relaxed a little now and asked in the manner of most patients: "But what *was* it that struck me down so violently? For I have never felt so low in my life."

"Your mama is a lady of the greatest good sense, and it is her view that it was a severe attack upon your nerves, exacerbated by the events which proceeded it. I made no deep enquiry into those, of course, but your parent, I collect, takes much of the blame upon herself and was most open about the fact."

"Yes, I know," acknowledged Merry, "but she was not wholly to blame—I did behave in the most aggravating manner, I'm sure."

"Well, it is not part of my commission to allot blame, is it, so we may leave that aspect!"

"Oh, no, I'm so sorry," said Almeria contritely. "It was quite improper of me to draw you into this affair in the first instance, but I shall be forever in your debt for your help," she concluded in a formal voice, at a loss as to what tone to adopt with him after this trying interview.

"Oh, but impropriety is no worry of yours, I thought!" Harry retorted in a quizzing way, but seeing his audience was not amused, he added, "You *still* don't really believe it, do you?"

"Yes, truly I do," she answered quickly, but it lacked conviction: she had never been skilled at dissembling.

Harry studied her open features for a moment and sighed. "Well, you leave me no alternative—I see I must play my trump card now! I had thought you might be so overset with joy that I would scarcely dare to add to your agitation so soon—but as it is . . ." He spread his hands and shrugged. "In short, Almeria, will you marry me?"

Merry may have looked composed throughout the preceding minutes, but she had been prey to the most conflicting emotions—now, her colour changed rapidly and she stared at Harry in a dazed fashion: it was too good to be true; there must be a prosaic reason for this offer—so out of character for Old Harry! "You've not the smallest need to feel sorry for me, you know! I daresay mama put it into your head to offer for me!" she said wildly.

"My dear girl, I have the utmost respect for your mama but no one shall direct *me* where to marry! What Mrs Denbury *did* put into my head was the notion that my quite unsolicited offer would meet with your unqualified approval—nay, even enthusiasm, I was given to understand." He looked at the uncertain face before him, and raised an eyebrow. "I must own it is a shade humbling to have one's first proposal in thirty years brushed aside! I had come to think there wasn't a maiden could resist me if only I were to ask—but there, it goes to show how one deceives oneself . . . At least I knew my rakish past could scarcely revolt you, with your delightfully refreshing attitude to scandalous behaviour!"

This nonsense gave Merry time to gather her wits. "You do mean it? Truly?"

"I do not care to answer such a paltry question," he said loftily. "I am waiting for *your* answer."

Instead of giving him a reply, she said: "Perhaps you should know why I made that rather indecorous visit to your home, first."

"Oh? What has that to say to anything? Not that I would not welcome an éclaircissement—but frankly I had quite despaired of ever obtaining one! However, does it signify at the moment, for I have no particular wish for diversions—be they wondrously entertaining."

"Oh yes, I believe it does!" She looked up at him with the most earnest expression, but then dropped her gaze before she continued, in a small voice: "You see I was quite set upon furthering my acquaintance with you, by any means at hand, so that I could broach the matter of becoming your mistress." She glanced up briefly. "Yes, it was quite shocking, I know, but you see I loved you desperately and yet marriage was out of the question— even had you been remotely interested in me—so it did seem the obvious solution."

"The devil it did!" cried Harry, part-amused, part-confounded. "I'm sorry I missed that encounter, I must say!"

"Oh, I'm perfectly sure I would have been rendered speechless had I been shown in to see you—"

"As indeed would I," murmured Harry.

"—But in the event the affair was the most dreadful bungle—and *then* I had to meet Major Maunby on your doorstep!"

"It wasn't such a bungle, you know," observed Harry, much struck, "for if you hadn't eavesdropped like that I should never have invited you to see *The Relapse,* and ergo, I should not have fallen in love with you! Well, not so soon, to be sure. And lord knows what state you would have fretted yourself into—or what wild escapades you would have fallen into, either, by that time!"

"You must mean it then, for if you love me, as you say, you would not look so cheerful if my days were limited," Merry deduced thoughtfully, as if she dared not let herself believe what was happening.

"At last I have convinced you, have I? All I can say is that if proposing is such difficult work I am glad I have not ventured upon it before—or, have to venture upon it again . . . will I?"

"No, of course you will not." Her sparkling eyes belied her calm tone.

"Then come here at once, you wicked baggage! If you were so set upon being my mistress the least you can do now is spare me a kiss!"

He took her by the hands and drew her up from the chair: Almeria's legs felt quite as weak as when she had first sat down, but for quite another reason . . .

"You know," said Harry, half to himself, "I believe we shall make a splendidly suitable ramshackle pair for Scantleby Hall."

But when Merry looked puzzled at this remark, he said impatiently: "Never mind, I'll explain later."

Harry was still chuckling to himself when he arrived back at Soho Square later that evening, and Tobin met him in the hall.

"Major Maunby is in the drawing-room, Sir Henry," Tobin announced.

"Is he, by Jove?" Harry said, rubbing his hands together, and going straight to his friend.

"How's this then, Cris, been thrown out, have you?"

"How could you say so, when I'm the apple of m'mother's eye?" Crispin retorted.

"Ay, maybe so, but it's father who does the throwing, is it not? Have you just arrived? Would you like a drink?"

"Yes, and yes, please! You're looking as self-satisfied as a cock with four spurs. Harry, what have you been up to in my absence? Something smoky, I'll be bound."

"*You* can answer a few questions first, I think," said Harry firmly, handing him a glass. "The first one being—why didn't you let me know you were coming back today?"

"Didn't know, old fellow, that's why. Only got my orders through last night."

"Orders?" Harry repeated, then with dawning realisation, he added, "You've been recalled to your regiment?"

"That's right—leave for France tomorrow. I'm joining the occupation army at the Duke of Wellington's headquarters at Cambray," he explained with a complacent smile.

"Dammit, Cris, that's marvellous! I am glad."

"Cost you a thousand pounds," Crispin reminded him. "I'm not taking a wife with me!"

"I'm still glad," reiterated Harry, undaunted. "And whose palm have you been greasing to achieve that?"

"Harry!" cried Crispin, "as if I would! . . . A crony of m'father's, actually, a friend of the Beau's. Well, pater saw the sense of it—with Meg Venables out of the running."

"Yes, when did you hear about her betrothal?"

Crispin grinned. "Had a letter the day before I left for home! Still, as I was saying, it made sense for me to get back on the King's Pay as soon as maybe, and the old codger was dashed helpful: dropped a word in the general's ear, and here we are—for the moment!"

"You deliberately tried to bamboozle me into thinking you were dangling after Mrs Wren, don't deny it!"

"No, why should I? Had to pay you back for trying to get me leg-shackled! Very unprincipled of you, that was, Harry!"

"Yes, I'm inclined to agree with you."

"Are you?" said Crispin, startled.

"Yes, I hold the view that only the worthiest and more admirable of us should venture on the path of matrimony. By the by," he went on, with a change of tone, "Cambray, you said? Well, I daresay we might call upon you when we are in Paris for our honeymoon."

"Honeymoon! Oh, capital! So *you're* to be the April-gentleman, after all. Hoist with your own petard, eh? . . . Who is it?" he asked belatedly.

"Almeria Denbury."

"Mm," said Crispin more soberly, considering this, "I'm not entirely surprised . . ."

"Well, I am, I can tell you!" laughed Harry.

Harry told Tobin the news the next day; and about a week later, as he went out, he informed him that he would be returning with his future wife and her mother to take some refreshment and see the house.

Now that he had had several days to become accustomed to it, Tobin was very pleased with the news of his master's forthcoming marriage; it depended upon who the lady was, of course, but whoever she was, she had had an inspiriting effect on Sir Henry, and Tobin couldn't regret that circumstance. He awaited the party's arrival with some impatience.

His smile of greeting suffered a slight set-back when he recognized the lady as the owner of the

phantom spaniel: it suffered an even greater check
when his master made the introductions.

". . . And this is Tobin, a most excellent man,
but you must forgive him at present if he seems a
trifle cast down. You see his lovely young Italian
wife, Rosa, has deserted him recently in the most
cruel fashion, to return to the land of her fathers."

Mrs Denbury showed but cursory interest in
Tobin's misfortunes, being more intent upon her
magnificent surroundings, but Almeria was inevitably reminded of that other alarming occasion
when she had set foot in this hall. Now, she glanced
at Harry with such an impudent twinkle in her eye
that for an uncomfortable moment he wondered
if she had guessed at Rosa's real identity—forgetting that he had no cause to worry about such
trifling past peccadilloes with a partner as worldly-
wise as Almeria . . .

Romantic Fiction

If you like novels of passion and daring adventure that take you to the very heart of human drama, these are the books for you.

☐ AFTER—Anderson	Q2279	1.50
☐ THE DANCE OF LOVE—Dodson	23110-0	1.75
☐ A GIFT OF ONYX—Kettle	23206-9	1.50
☐ TARA'S HEALING—Giles	23012-0	1.50
☐ THE DEFIANT DESIRE—Klem	13741-4	1.75
☐ LOVE'S TRIUMPHANT HEART—Ashton	13771-6	1.75
☐ MAJORCA—Dodson	13740-6	1.75

Buy them at your local bookstores or use this handy coupon for ordering:

FAWCETT BOOKS GROUP
P.O. Box C730, 524 Myrtle Ave., Pratt Station, Brooklyn, N.Y. 11205

Please send me the books I have checked above. Orders for less than 5 books must include 75¢ for the first book and 25¢ for each additional book to cover mailing and handling. I enclose $_____ in check or money order.

Name_____
Address_____
City_____State/Zip_____
Please allow 4 to 5 weeks for delivery.

Victoria Holt

Over 20,000,000 copies of Victoria Holt's novels are in print.
If you have missed any of her spellbinding bestsellers, here
is an opportunity to order any or all direct by mail.

☐ BRIDE OF PENDORRIC	23280-8	1.95
☐ THE CURSE OF THE KINGS	23284-0	1.95
☐ THE HOUSE OF A THOUSAND		
LANTERNS	23685-4	1.95
☐ THE KING OF THE CASTLE	23587-4	1.95
☐ KIRKLAND REVELS	X2917	1.75
☐ THE LEGEND OF THE SEVENTH VIRGIN	23281-6	1.95
☐ LORD OF THE FAR ISLAND	22874-6	1.95
☐ MENFREYA IN THE MORNING	23757-5	1.95
☐ MISTRESS OF MELLYN	23124-0	1.75
☐ ON THE NIGHT OF THE SEVENTH MOON	23568-0	1.95
☐ THE QUEENS' CONFESSION	23213-1	1.95
☐ THE SECRET WOMAN	23283-2	1.95
☐ THE SHADOW OF THE LYNX	23278-6	1.95
☐ THE SHIVERING SANDS	23282-4	1.95

Buy them at your local bookstores or use this handy coupon for ordering: